COME TO ME

A Dare With Me Novel

J.H. CROIX

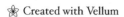

DEDICATION

"What hurts you, blesses you. Darkness is your candle." -Rumi

Sign up for my newsletter for information on new releases & get a FREE copy of one of my books!

http://jhcroixauthor.com/subscribe/

Follow me!
   jhcroix@jhcroix.com
   https://amazon.com/author/jhcroix
   https://www.bookbub.com/authors/j-h-croix
   https://www.facebook.com/jhcroix
   https://www.instagram.com/jhcroix/

Chapter One

GEMMA

My breath came in ragged bursts as I jogged across the gravel parking lot. "Charlie!" I hollered.

My horse twitched his tail and picked up his pace from a trot to a canter. "You little shit," I muttered. It's not like I could easily catch up to him, but I needed to catch him and hoped he tired of his antics soon. I kept going, cursing when I stubbed my toe on a giant rock and hoping Charlie didn't keep going and end up near the highway in Diamond Creek.

Diamond Creek, Alaska wasn't all that busy. With the exception of the summer months when the traffic on the highway was bumper to bumper with RVs. I heard the rumble of a motorcycle behind me and hoped the driver was paying close attention. I saw Charlie's tail rise in the air as he turned and looked back, his mane lifting and rippling with a gust of wind.

The motorcycle passed me carefully and then slowed. I presumed when they saw my escaped horse. The stirrups were flopping as Charlie finally came to a stop and looked back toward me.

"Charlie!" I called.

Although I was in decent shape, I was running out of breath, figuring I'd run at least two miles now and definitely faster than I preferred. I stopped, resting my hands on my knees. Just then, I heard the rumble of a motorcycle approaching from the opposite direction this time.

"Oh, no," I muttered to myself.

Lifting my head, I was relieved to see the motorcyclist slowing as they passed by Charlie. I began walking again, immediately breaking into a jog. The motorcycle slowed beside me. The guy driving it called over, "Is that your horse?"

I nodded and kept on jogging. I didn't really know why this guy was asking. I couldn't see if it was anyone I knew. I didn't know that many people yet in Diamond Creek, with the exception of the students who had begun coming to my yoga classes and the staff at my favorite new coffee shop.

The man on the motorcycle came to a stop and carefully turned his bike around again. Glancing over my shoulder a few seconds later, I saw him rolling to a stop beside me. Then, the man opened the visor on his motorcycle helmet, and I recognized Diego Jackson.

The moment my eyes landed on him, my belly spun in several rapid somersaults. Of all the men to stop, it just had to be Diego.

My hormones let out a little cheer. I'd met Diego a few times. He'd come to some of my yoga classes with his friend, Flynn, who dragged him and some other guys along whenever Flynn's girlfriend wanted Flynn to come with her. Those men were dripping with testosterone and enough hotness to melt panties. Of course, only one man sent my body into overdrive—Diego.

"Hey, Gemma. Hop on," Diego said, patting the seat behind him. "I promise I won't go too fast, and you're wearing a helmet." He pointed to my riding helmet.

I hesitated, but then glanced ahead to see Charlie's tail flick in the air as he took off at a fast trot. There was no way I was going to catch him on foot.

"Are you sure you don't mind?" I hedged, wondering if I could even handle climbing on a motorcycle behind Diego and being pressed up against all of that muscled hardness.

I didn't know Diego drove a motorcycle, but then I didn't know much about him at all. Other than that he had a body worthy of sculpture, and he flew planes.

"I'm positive. Don't take this the wrong way, but I don't think you can catch that horse on foot. He's not in town yet, but he's getting close, and then we'll be dealing with traffic."

I was a reasonable woman, and I knew he had a point. I didn't hesitate any further, and climbed on behind Diego. I ignored the flutters in my belly and the heat pinwheeling like hot sparks through me.

"Put your arms around me," he ordered.

I wrapped my arms around his waist. Diego wore a leather jacket, which didn't do much to mask the fact that his body was all muscle. My pulse drummed out an excited beat.

"I won't go too fast," he called over his shoulder as he put his bike in gear.

The engine rumbled under my thighs. I'd never actually ridden on a motorcycle. I felt the vibration through my entire body while he eased the speed up slowly.

In less than a minute, we caught up to my naughty

horse. I'd only had Charlie for a few months. He was a beauty, with a dappled gray coat and an elegant build. I planned to pull his mane soon, but I loved the way it flowed in the wind, as it did now.

His bridle jingled from the reins flapping, and the stirrups slapped against his sides. He glanced sideways and let out a little snort. I felt Diego's chuckle reverberate through his body.

"He thinks this is funny," I offered over Diego's shoulder.

Charlie dodged and picked up his pace when I reached for the reins. Further demonstrating just how funny he thought he was, he glanced back at Diego's motorcycle, letting out another little snort when Diego caught up to his side again.

This time, Diego was lightning fast and grabbed the reins, slowing his bike smoothly while keeping a firm hold of Charlie. He eased to the side of the road, and Charlie had enough sense to follow. We stopped on the shoulder, and I carefully climbed off the motorcycle. I took the reins from Diego.

"Thank you, I don't think I would've gotten him soon without your help."

Diego lifted his visor again, removing his helmet and running a hand through his dark curls. His hair was ruffled, and his green eyes scanned from Charlie to me while my pulse took off like a rocket. My hormones did a little happy dance.

The gods and goddesses of beauty had been generous with Diego. His eyes were like a forest filled with secrets, mossy green and intense. They stood out in a face that was already too much with a jaw that could cut glass, a sensual mouth, and cheekbones that could make a sculptor weep. Also, he was strong, like ridiculously muscular.

I was usually in a pretty good mental space when I taught yoga, but whenever he showed up, my hormones went wild in my body. He wore these fitted T-shirts and gym shorts that did nothing to disguise his great ass, his honed shoulders, arms, thighs and calves. His *everything*. I was pretty sure even his toes could rev my hormones.

Diego's gaze bounced back to Charlie. "He's a beauty."

I nodded, glancing back to my horse. "A beauty and a handful." Charlie nuzzled his head into my shoulder, and I scrubbed behind his ears.

"How far do you need to go to get him home?"

I gestured over my shoulder. "A few miles back that way. I don't live on this road, but on a side road. Thank you again. He was getting too close to town for my comfort."

"Did he throw you off?"

I sighed. "Yes. He's a little rambunctious. I don't think I can ride him outside of the pasture again. Not yet."

Diego chuckled, and butterflies twirled in my belly. Sweet hell. This man just did it for me, and it was all rather unsettling.

"So, you're a yoga teacher and a horse rider. What else don't I know about you?" he asked, his mouth kicking up at the corners in a smile that sent liquid fire spinning through my veins.

I felt a little breathless. "That's pretty much it."

"Why don't I follow you home, in case he's feeling rambunctious again?"

I was about to say no when I realized that wasn't the best choice. By the time Charlie had unseated me, he had shied twice. The last thing I wanted was to dismiss Diego's offer and find myself chasing my horse again.

"You don't mind?"

"If I minded, I wouldn't have offered.

"All right, then."

I mounted Charlie. After checking to see Diego had already pulled his visor down and was waiting, I gave Charlie a light squeeze with my calves, and he shifted into a trot. Conveniently, Charlie didn't seem bothered by the sound of a motorcycle rumbling behind us, but then Diego kept the engine low and rode at a comfortable distance.

Not much later, I slowed to a walk and brought Charlie into the small barn. I waved over my shoulder, calling, "Thank you," to Diego.

I quickly took off Charlie's saddle and bridle, slipping on his halter. After brushing him, I put him in his stall with some fresh hay and water. All in all, that took maybe five minutes.

I didn't expect to find Diego waiting, but his motorcycle was still there when I walked back out. He had removed his helmet and appeared to be on the phone.

With my pulse thrumming along and those butterflies spinning madly in my belly again, I approached him because it seemed rude to ignore him. Without his help, Charlie very well may have ended up facing traffic, which could've been a disaster.

"Got it," Diego said into his phone. "I'll be back soon."

Lowering the phone, he glanced over at me. His helmet was resting on his lap. Dear God, he was just *all* man, sitting on that motorcycle in faded jeans and that leather jacket.

"Is Charlie all safe and sound now?" he asked.

I nodded because it was all I could manage. My brain cells had imploded just looking at him and words required too much effort. I watched as his eyes scanned the barn and the adjoining pasture before circling around to the small house across the grass on the other side of the gravel area.

I'd lucked into this job and rental. The owners had moved away and needed someone to take care of the horses. There were four horses, two of which they owned. They rented out stalls for two other horses. I got paid to take care of the horses, and I got to ride one of them myself. The house rental came as part of the deal at a very reduced rate. All in all, this gig made it possible for me to make the leap in moving to Alaska and bought me time to get my yoga teaching business off the ground.

When I'd won an all-expenses-paid trip to Alaska and fallen in love with it, I wondered how I could make it work to live here. This situation gave me a soft landing.

"Beautiful place," he commented.

Just beyond the house was an opening through the trees that offered a view of the mountains and the sparkling harbor in the distance. "Hard not to have a beautiful view here," I replied.

His eyes crinkled at the corners with his grin. "Very true." He glanced to the mountains before bringing his gaze back to me. "I should be going. I suppose I might see you in yoga class sometime."

"Come as often as you like."

His mouth kicked up at one corner. "Now, Gemma, are you scolding me for not being a more consistent student?"

The teasing hint in his tone sent a wash of heat through my body. I felt my cheeks getting hot and shrugged. "Of course not. I know you guys come because Daphne and Cammi talk you into it," I said, referring to the respective girlfriends of two of his friends.

Diego threw his head back with a laugh. "Maybe so, but I always enjoy it when I'm there."

Chapter Two

DIEGO

Gemma Marlon stood in front of me, her fingers rubbing the hem of her T-shirt with one hand while she held the strap of her riding helmet in the other, swinging it lightly. She seemed a little nervous. Considering how she set my nerves alight and the sizzle of chemistry between us, I wondered if that had her unsettled.

That chemistry created a fizzy sensation inside with raw desire sizzling through my body. I'd met her when Flynn had dragged a few of us with him to yoga class when Daphne wanted him to go.

Considering my friends here were like family, I gamely went along with him. I thought I'd have to suffer through it, but there was no suffering involved. The second I clapped eyes on Gemma, I didn't want to leave. She was a quirky kind of beautiful with a sensual, throaty voice that nearly undid me. I didn't think she meant for me to be so turned on in every class that it was an act of will to keep my body in check.

She let go of the hem of her T-shirt and lifted her

hand to sift her fingers through her ruffled curls. She had rumpled honey-gold curls. They fell to her shoulders, making me want to brush them away and dust kisses on her neck.

I paused, taking the moment to absorb her. She had big brown eyes paired with her curls. Despite the cool Alaskan summer, her skin was sun-kissed, like honey. She was on the short side with a toned body that was somehow inviting and curvy at the same time. She'd fit nicely behind me on my motorcycle, her thighs curving around mine. I'd wanted to spin around and kiss her senseless.

We stared at each other for several long seconds, and I marveled that she was comfortable with the quiet.

After a moment, she added, "I bet you get to see the best of Alaska."

I'd actually lost the thread of our conversation. "What do you mean?"

"Because you fly, so you get to see everything from above," she explained, gesturing to the sky, which was blue today with fluffy clouds scudding across its surface as the wind had started to pick up.

"Have you flown since you've been here?"

She shook her head quickly, her curls bouncing. "I took a plane to get here, but that's it."

"Well, then, I'll take you. Coming in on a commercial flight doesn't give you the kind of view you can get in the smaller planes."

"You will?" she squeaked.

"Of course." I felt my phone vibrate in my chest pocket over my heart. "I actually need to go." That vibration was the alarm I'd set to let me know when it was time to head out to the plane hangar for a scheduled flight. "Not today, but give me your number," I said, sliding my phone out. "I'll text you when I've got a free day to take you."

"Isn't that kind of expensive?"

"You're not paying."

Gemma started to shake her head, and I shook mine harder in return. "Seriously. Give me your number," I repeated.

After she recited it, I punched it in and sent her a quick text. "Just so you have mine. Now, I gotta roll." I slipped on my helmet.

"Thank you again!" she called as I started my motorcycle.

With a wave, I drove off. The distance from her place out to the small airport in Diamond Creek was short. There was a commercial airport here, but I was aiming for the one where small planes, which were serious business in Alaska, were housed in a collection of hangars lining the runway. I flew planes for one of my best friends. Flynn Walker owned and ran an outdoor resort in the wilderness, twenty miles, give or take, from Diamond Creek proper. They served guests for a variety of outdoor activities, along with guided plane trips.

I'd met Flynn when we were in the Air Force together and would lay my life on the line for the man. So far, there were four of us who'd moved here after he let us know we could make good money. It was a dream job. I loved to fly planes, and Alaska was flat out beautiful, the kind of beauty that elicited a sense of awe.

After my time in the Air Force, I'd needed a place where I could land and do what I did best, and Alaska turned out to be exactly what I needed. Some of my best friends in life, close enough to call family in my heart, were here, and I got to live and work with them.

Diamond Creek was a small town, but it catered to tourists, so there was good food and decent shopping, if that was your thing. I didn't care so much for the shopping, but I sure as hell cared for the food and the people.

I made it to the hangar just in time. While I rounded up the family I was taking for a scenic jaunt, I made a mental note to check the schedule and text Gemma when I had a free day. I wouldn't mind more than a free day with Gemma.

———

Grant tossed a five-dollar bill toward his older brother, Flynn, and rolled his eyes. "There you go. You win."

Flynn swiped the money from the table with a chuckle. "Don't worry, you know you'll win it back."

I grinned at Grant. "You absolutely will. Flynn's lost his touch at cards ever since he and Daphne got together."

Flynn cuffed me lightly on the shoulder where he sat beside me on the couch. "I'm not that bad."

Tucker, who sat across from me on the other side of the sectional, cast Flynn a knowing look. "Hell, yeah, you are. It's all right. We're all happy for you. Plus, I've been winning more lately."

"It's not like we play for much money, guys," I offered as Flynn gathered the cards and began to shuffle them.

I'd been working here going on four years now. Flynn owned Walker Adventures with his younger brother, Grant, the very one who was giving him a little hell, and his younger sister Nora. I supposed Cat counted too, but she was only seventeen. Their mother had started the resort with Flynn's stepfather, although it had never really gotten off the ground. After they'd both passed away within a few years of each other, Flynn had left the Air Force to come home and take care of his siblings. Flynn was the oldest of the four, the only one who didn't share the same father. He'd been in the Air Force with me, Tucker, and Elias, who didn't happen to be here with us tonight. He was all but officially shacked up with his girlfriend, Cammi.

"I think I'm past the honeymoon stage with Daphne," Flynn commented as he began to deal out the cards. "I'm not nearly as bad as Elias."

"True," Grant said with a solemn nod. "Both of you are definitely more cheerful."

"Speaking of cheerful, where the hell is Gabriel?" I asked.

"Since when was Gabriel cheerful?" Tucker chimed in with a slow grin.

"He had the last flight on the schedule today and said he was going to do some quick repairs on that plane that's been acting up," Flynn replied.

Tucker caught my eyes, but I held my silence. I didn't doubt Gabriel was actually doing those repairs. Like all of us, during our time in the military as pilots we'd also been trained as plane mechanics. But I suspected he was doing more than repairs. Considering that Nora hadn't been at dinner at the resort tonight either, my suspicion was she was helping Gabriel. Those two were either at each other's throats... Or, trying to hide the fact that they were tangled up in the sheets on occasion. Whatever their arrangement was, it ran in fits and starts. Flynn had to suspect, but then maybe he had a blind spot because he was so focused on Daphne lately.

Our game carried on. We'd picked up the habit of

doing this at least once a week. It was something we'd done when we were in the military together. Although Elias was mostly staying with Cammi these days, even he made a point to come out every other week or so.

After one more round, Flynn was getting up to leave when he glanced around. "Who's coming to yoga tomorrow?"

Flynn stayed in a private area at the main resort with Daphne and his sister, Cat. Grant, Tucker, Gabriel, and I shared this house that we'd built together only two summers ago. Elias still officially had a bedroom, but he didn't use it anymore.

Tucker snorted a laugh. "Dude, not me."

Grant let out a sigh. "I'll go. Last time I didn't go, Daphne asked me about it."

All of us had a hard time telling Daphne "no" to anything she asked. She fed us so well ever since she'd become the chef at the resort that we all kind of felt like we had to do something for her.

"I'll be there," I offered. I wanted to see Gemma again. Although, yoga did actually feel good.

Tucker chuckled. "I guess I'm not as susceptible to guilt. I love Daphne's food, and I thank her effusively every meal. Plus, you pay her, right?" Tucker asked, looking genuinely horrified at the prospect that Flynn might not be paying her to do her job.

"Of course, I pay her." Flynn looked affronted at the mere implication he might not be.

"Dude, you have one job. Keep Daphne happy, all right?" Tucker teased. "Now that you two are in love, we have to worry about drama shit."

"No need to worry about that," Flynn said firmly. "Now, I'll see you guys tomorrow."

"When's Aubrey moving up here?" I asked Tucker after the door closed behind Flynn.

"She says sometime next year. She's got her pilot's license and everything. Not sure how I feel about having my sister here, but Flynn says we can always use another pilot."

"Dude, I have to deal with two sisters and my older brother as a boss," Grant said. "You can deal with one sister."

Tucker chuckled. "Fair enough."

His eyes caught mine. "How are your sisters?"

I was the oldest of five with four younger sisters. I was up to my eyeballs in dealing with women. My family was tight, real tight. It's just none of us were in the same place. My dad had been in the Air Force, and we were all military kids, used to bouncing all over the place. My dad had since passed on, and so had my mom. We missed them both like crazy, and I talked to my sisters without fail several times a week.

"They're all good. Every week, there's something to deal with. None of them are pilots, so I don't need to worry about them coming up here to work with us. You know everybody will be up for a visit at some point, maybe not all at the same time though."

"It's a good thing you all get along," Grant offered.

"Define 'get along,'" I said dryly.

We loved each other, but we were known to argue. To a fault, no one in our family held back when it came to expressing feelings.

"Remind me where you're from?" Grant prompted.

While Grant was a pilot, he hadn't been in the Air Force with us. He was seven years younger than Flynn.

"All over the place. I was born in Texas, but my dad signed up for the military and we bounced around. We made it back to Texas later when my dad was stationed there. That's where I finished high school. Because both my parents were fluent in Spanish, along with the rest of us, he got a good job as a translator after he retired from the military. After that, he started his own construction business. It worked out really well for him."

"How do you like Alaska then? It's a far cry from Texas."

I shrugged. "It is, but when you're a military brat, you get used to being in different places. I might've been born in Texas, but we left by the time I hit first grade. I suppose I know the state well because we made it back there later on, but home is more of a feeling than a place for me. I love Alaska. It's beautiful, and I've got you guys. Y'all are family just as much as my sisters are."

Speaking of sisters, my phone rang then. I glanced at the screen. "It's Harley. I better take this, or she'll give me hell," I commented.

The guys chuckled as I stood and walked into the kitchen to take the call. "Hey, sis."

"Hey, can I come visit?" my sister asked, getting right to the point, as she was wont to do.

"You know you're always welcome. What's going on?"

"I just dumped Joey, and I need a place to stay. There's no fucking way I'm going back to that job to stare at his face anymore. So, I quit my job too. I thought maybe I could crash up there for a while and figure out what I want to do next," Harley explained.

Harley had a touch of a temper, not the bad kind, but the quick kind. She never pitched a fit. She made fast decisions and acted on them immediately when she was upset.

I thought about Elias's empty bedroom upstairs. "You're welcome to stay. Give me a heads up on when you'll be here."

"It'll be in a few weeks. I'm gonna go stay with Terese for two weeks," she explained, referring to another one of our sisters. "I haven't seen her in a bit and then I'll come up there."

"That'll work."

"Perfect. Love you."

The line clicked in my ear the second I said, "Love you too."

Shaking my head with a laugh, I stared at the phone in my hand and took a breath. I loved my youngest sister, but sometimes she stirred things up. She also *always* had an opinion on my life. It would be interesting to have her here.

Chapter Three

GEMMA

I took a bite of the scone and a subtle orange flavor broke across my tongue. "Oh, my God," I moaned, my words coming out muffled because I was chewing. I moaned again and swallowed. Leveling my gaze with Cammi's, I said, "This is amazing. I thought you said baking wasn't your forte."

Cammi smiled, her blue eyes twinkling. "It's not. I set up a gig with Daphne out at the resort. She's going to do a rotation of baked goods for me since they have room in the kitchen out there. She's incredible. We've even got a plan for delivery with the guys who come to fly every day. Between them, somebody comes to town every single day. They drop them off for me the afternoon before, and I pop them in the oven the next morning."

"Wow. I already thought your coffee was incredible, but now with this, you're taking it to the next level." I meant every word. I'd discovered Misty Mountain Café on my second day in town, and I loved it.

Cammi beamed. "Thank you. Really. Like I told

you, before this year my only expertise was coffee. I've got coffee down to a science. Taking this place over is a big step for me, and I knew I needed to up my food game."

"You've given up doing massage?" I asked, referring to the side job Cammi told me she did occasionally in the winters for the physical therapy clinic at the hospital.

"Yeah, I had to. There's no way for me to fit it in. Is that something you do? I mean, you teach yoga so..." Her words trailed off. Her honey brown hair bounced as she nodded, as if she was answering herself.

"I don't do massage," I offered with a smile. "I want to focus on my yoga classes. That, and the horse stuff. I love spending time with animals, and it's working out to be a pretty sweet set up for me."

"You gotta do what fits for you. Do you plan to stay in Diamond Creek long term?" she asked as she prepped the coffee I'd ordered before giving me the sample scone to taste.

"I'm hoping to stay. I wasn't sure if I'd have enough business. I'm realizing if I do double duty in the summer, there are plenty of tourists who want to sign up for yoga classes while they're here. In the winter, I can charge monthly fees for the locals and maybe some extra things on top of that. I love it here."

"Diamond Creek's a good place. I grew up here, so I might sound biased. Even though it feels like it's the middle of nowhere, we've got good restaurants and plenty of shopping. There's a small town vibe with a touch of the city."

Turning, I looked out the windows of the small café, which offered a view of the mountains and the ocean bay sparkling under the sunshine. "I wouldn't say city as far as the view goes, but as far as the restaurants and the coffee, hell yes. Now, I've got a morning yoga class, so I'll catch you later."

Cammi blew me a kiss and waved as I turned away, calling, "I'll see you for the evening class."

On my drive to the yoga studio, my phone rang. My car dashboard indicated it was my mother. I took a deep breath. Although I loved my mother, calls from her did, in fact, require deep breathing techniques on occasion.

Tapping the button to take the call, I said, "Hey, Mom."

"Gemma, how's Alaska?"

"It's still great, Mom. Just like I told you three days ago."

My mother's sigh filtered through the car speakers. "I know, sweetie. You're a long way away, and I'm still getting used to that."

"I know, Mom. It's not as far as you think. Portland's a four-hour plane trip away."

"I know, I know. We miss you."

I turned my car onto the road that led to my yoga studio. "I miss you too. I'd love it if you all came up to visit soon. The weather's gorgeous here in the summer."

"I'll talk with your father and see what his work schedule looks like. I hope you're making friends."

I bit back a sigh. God bless my mother. She worried about me. But then, she was a worrier. "I promise I'm making friends. I've got a class in just a few minutes, so I need to go. I'll call you this weekend, okay?"

"All right, sweetie. Love you."

"Love you too."

With the tap of a button on my dashboard, I

ended the call. As I turned into the parking lot, I took another breath and ordered myself not to feel guilty about moving away. I was blessed with two loving parents and an older brother who was also awesome. The cliché that family could be complicated rang so true in my life. Love only added another layer to the complications.

I wouldn't describe myself as the black sheep of my family, but maybe the gray sheep. I didn't quite fit, and I'd struggled with feeling like a disappointment. Both of my parents were brilliant. Both of my parents were highly successful lawyers.

Meanwhile, my brother was a star student, valedictorian of his high school class, blasting through college in three years and finishing law school in another two. He did everything at double speed. It was hard to follow in his footsteps. My parents never seemed to know what to do with me because school hadn't come as easily for me as them. They didn't know what to do and didn't bother to get an assessment. They'd been confused about why I was struggling in school when I was younger. When they finally did get me tested and discovered I had dyslexia, things were much better, but then I was playing catch up and still saddled with the frustration of the situation.

I never quite got over feeling like such a disappointment. Fortunately, I excelled at sports. Softball was my thing, and I'd been a high school star, until my coach took a shine to me and a few other girls on the team. It's not all that fun to be a statistic—yet another teenage girl fending off inappropriate sexual advances from an adult coach.

My parents didn't know how to fix that little mess. All in all, between the situation with my coach and then injuring my back the following year, my promising college sports career collapsed. The saving grace was I found yoga to help with my injury. I loved it, and I loved teaching classes. Between that and riding horses, another holdover from childhood and a bright spot, I carved my own path, a path that led me to Alaska by chance.

Now, my parents acted like I was a million miles away and took it a little personally that I'd chosen to move away from Portland. They felt guilt for not understanding my struggles earlier, all of it compounded by what happened with my coach. I knew they genuinely didn't expect me to change who I was for them, but it had become this tangled, messy baggage in the aftermath of how things played out. For reasons I couldn't easily articulate, I knew I needed the distance and a fresh start to find my footing in life. Alaska was giving me that.

I hurried into my yoga studio, casting a quick look around. It was a shared rental space that hosted my yoga classes, exercise classes for physical therapy patients, and dance classes. I loved the space as it was open and bright with a beautiful view out the windows toward the mountains.

Students started trickling in not long after I got everything set up and unlocked the doors. I found that the morning group tended to be the students who were serious and wanted to start their days with yoga. I loved it because it got me to start my day that way too.

My day was busy between my morning class and then heading home to let the horses out into the pasture and do some training with Charlie. After my mishap, I wasn't riding him outside of the fenced area. I was working with him in the small lunging ring. He had basic training, but his spunky personality meant he needed more work to curb some bad habits.

My other job was doing freelance graphic design work. I'd started doing it in Portland for friends on occasion. It wasn't anything I ever wanted to do full-time, because I couldn't imagine sitting at the computer for that long, but I enjoyed making signs and promotional materials. It was a steady supplemental income and a great contrast to my other work. Today, after I finished up, I worked on some small graphics for myself to post locally, promoting my yoga classes to tourists

After that, I returned to town for my evening yoga class. The first to arrive: Diego with the crew from the resort. Today's group included Diego, Grant, Flynn and Daphne, along with Elias and Cammi. This group of men was supercharged with testosterone and sexiness. But then, Alaska men seemed supercharged in general, carrying themselves with an easy type of masculinity, not from working out, but from living rugged lives where they stayed active.

When Diego crossed over to collect a mat from the shelves on the wall, he stopped beside me. "I hope you haven't gotten thrown off again."

When I met his eyes, his mouth kicked up at one corner, sending my belly into a series of wild flips. I shook my head. "Oh, no. I don't think I'll be taking Charlie on the road again for a while. He has a rambunctious streak."

"Clearly," Diego replied with a solemn face. I didn't miss the teasing glint in his eyes, and my pulse revved in response.

I was blessedly distracted by another student. I

started the class, telling myself over and over not to spend too much time focusing on Diego. I made a habit of moving around the room whenever I taught class, but I found my eyes lingering on him, again and again and *again*. It didn't help that the man was practically a living, breathing sculpture.

After class, I was chatting with Cammi and Daphne when Daphne said, "You should come."

"Come to what?" I asked.

"The grand opening."

"Reopening," Cammi corrected, her cheeks flushing slightly. "Now that it's been a few months, and I've had time to put my stamp on Misty Mountain, I'm doing a grand reopening this weekend."

"We'll all be there," Elias said as he stopped beside us.

"Of course, you will," I teased.

Elias curled his arm around Cammi's shoulders, speaking to the room at large, "Anyone you know, round them up."

When Diego and Flynn meandered over, Daphne smiled between them. "Flynn's coming."

"If you didn't notice yet, Flynn goes anywhere you want him to go," Diego teased with a warm smile.

Daphne's cheeks went a little pink as her gaze arced over to him. "You'll be there, right?"

"Absolutely," he said. "Wouldn't miss it. Plus, you told me I had to go."

Daphne rolled her eyes. "I hope you're going because you want to be there."

"Of course. I know there will be amazing coffee. I also hear there will be alcohol and your food. I wouldn't miss it," Diego said firmly.

When Daphne cast me a questioning glanced, I chimed in, "I'll be there."

Chapter Four

DIEGO

I wanted to linger after yoga class. Hell, I hadn't even really wanted to go to yoga class, but I went because it meant I got to see Gemma. Gemma in a fitted tank top and leggings sent lust sizzling through me. I wasn't certain, but I thought she avoided me a little during the class, only giving me two gentle corrections.

That's how ridiculous I was. There I was, hoping I'd need her help during class, anything to get me close to her no matter how brief. As we were walking out to the parking lot, Daphne asked, "Did I hear your sister was coming up to Alaska to stay for a while?"

I slid my gaze to her and nodded. "I figure with Elias at Cammi's place all the time, she can have his bedroom. That okay?" I looked to Flynn as we collectively paused in the parking lot beside his truck.

"Of course," he replied. "As long as it's okay with Elias."

"As long as what's okay?" Elias asked when he stopped beside us.

"My sister is coming up to stay. Can she stay in your bedroom?"

"You're at Cammi's all the time anyway," Grant observed with a sly grin.

Elias glanced to Cammi. "That okay with you? That means I'll really be at your place all the time."

Cammi smiled up at him, her cheeks pinkening slightly. "Yes."

"Might as well make it official and just move your stuff out of the room," I teased.

"I'll definitely clean it up for your sister," he countered with a laugh rustling in his throat. With that, he waved and left with Cammi. I climbed in my truck, following Flynn's truck home.

Grant rode back to the resort with me. "Feeling all mellow?" he asked as I turned onto the highway that led us out of Diamond Creek.

I chuckled. "Actually, I am. I thought it was a joke when Flynn wanted us to go to these classes because Daphne asked him, but after a day of sitting in a plane, it feels good to stretch out." I kept my silence on how good it was to see Gemma.

"Agreed."

"This view still hasn't gotten old," I commented, looking ahead to the mountains rising in the distance with the waters of the bay glittering under the setting sun to one side and the lush greenery of the Alaskan forest on the other.

"It never does," Grant replied. "I've been here my whole life, and I still love it."

We fell quiet after that. One of the things I liked about hanging out with Grant was he didn't mind silence. I was feeling relaxed and loose and soaked in the view on the stunning drive home. Living in Alaska sometimes felt like living in a postcard.

Walker Adventures, the resort Flynn owned with

his brother and sisters was roughly twenty minutes outside of Diamond Creek, down a long gravel road. It was far enough out that if you didn't know Diamond Creek was nearby, you could imagine you were completely isolated. As the crow flew, you were. The little town gave us an outlet, and also made this resort's booming business possible. People could come for the wilderness expeditions and go to town for shopping, food, and the summer crowds.

"Wonder what Daphne's got lined up for dinner," Grant commented as I rolled to a stop in the parking lot outside the main resort.

"No matter what it is, it'll be delicious," I replied as we climbed out together and crossed the parking lot.

Grant chuckled. "That's a guarantee."

We climbed the stairs to the large building. The resort was a three-story octagonal shape. The main guest area was spacious and offered several areas for gathering. One area had a fireplace with seating around it, another had a large flatscreen television mounted on the wall with more seating, and yet another area had bookshelves and seating.

There was only one guest room on the main floor, in addition to the living room area, the kitchen and dining area, and the family's private apartment. The upper floors were all guest rooms. Winter was a little quieter, but once we hit spring, it was like horses taking off for a race. We were full speed ahead with guests flowing in and out every week. In addition to leading hikes and other outdoor activities, the resort offered private sightseeing flights daily from spring through early winter. We continued flying during winter, but the pace was much slower.

With Flynn leading the group, there were currently seven pilots. Flynn, Grant, Elias, Gabriel, Tucker, Nora, and me. Tucker's sister, Aubrey, had her pilot's license and would be joining us at some point. Flynn had recently bought another plane and absorbed the operations from a local pilot, giving us even more customers. We rotated between taking guests out for scenic flights, which were pricey, and also providing transport for goods and mail amongst several communities in the area.

As a pilot, it was pure heaven—amazing views and never boring. I loved it. Coming out of the Air Force, I couldn't have imagined landing a job like this. It turned out that being one of Flynn's closest friends was a blessing in more ways than one.

It wasn't always easy though. Flying in Alaska was definitely high on the risk quotient between the weather and small planes. Just last autumn, Flynn and Elias had been in a small plane crash. They'd come out okay, although Elias had broken his ankle badly and been on crutches for a bit. I would take the risk, just for the peace of mind it gave me to be doing what I loved in such an incredible place.

Once we were inside the resort, we encountered guests milling about in the common area. Grant and I cut straight through into the kitchen. The dining here had gone from decent to fantastic over the last year. Daphne had come out for a stay at the resort last fall. She was a true chef, like big-time back in Atlanta. Flynn could be a hell of a boss with the chefs, and she'd stepped in to help after another one quit. Conveniently, she and Flynn fell in love and she stayed in Alaska. He had enough sense to give her full rein of the kitchen, so we all benefitted.

Cat, the youngest of the Walker siblings at seventeen, was hard at work at the stove when we entered the kitchen. I stopped beside her, peering down. "Oh, that smells freaking great. Do you need some help?"

Cat quickly stirred some vegetables with strips of beef in the pan as she glanced to me. "Do you want to check the rice? Daphne's got something going in the oven too."

Crossing over, I checked the rice steamer. The rice was done, so I set to work seasoning it. Daphne came hurrying out of the pantry with her auburn hair up in a bun. She smiled over at me. "Thank you! You're a godsend, Diego."

I'd always loved to cook. Daphne trusted me enough to help out now that she'd learned I had a clue in the kitchen. Not much later, I was sitting with the staff at the island counter, while Daphne served the guests at the massive dining table by the windows. When the crowd was thinner, staff would sometimes sit over there. When Daphne didn't serve dinner for the guests, staff lounged at the table for dinner, drinks and lazy chatter.

I leaned back in my stool and let out a sigh. "Damn, that was good."

Cat smiled over at me. She shared the same coloring as Flynn and Grant, gray eyes with dark blond hair.

"That stir fry is good stuff. I taste ginger in there," I added.

Cat's ponytail bounced as she nodded. "Good guess."

Nora smiled at her. "You're a blessing for Daphne. Flynn and I can't cook." Of the Walker siblings, Nora was the only one with brown hair and brown eyes.

Grant cast a sheepish smile. "Me neither."

Cat ducked her head, her cheeks flushing with her smile. "I love cooking, and Daphne's the best teacher."

"What's the schedule tomorrow?" I asked Nora.

She'd been working on it earlier. She pulled her laptop closer on the counter and opened it, tapping a key and bringing the screen to life. "We've got two delivery trips for mail and groceries, and we've got four scenic flights scheduled for guests." She glanced to me, her eyes taking on a gleam. "You should take that group of women. One of them has her eyes on you."

"I'll pass then," I replied quickly.

Nora's brows hitched up. "You're a professional flirt."

I shrugged. "Not in the mood for flirting right now," I said lightly.

Tucker caught my eyes from where he sat across from me. "Dude, what gives?"

"Nothing, how about I take one of the deliveries?"

"One of them includes a rescue dog being adopted, so we'll be transporting it over," Nora offered.

"I'll take that one. The dog can ride in the front with me," I offered.

Nora tapped it into the schedule. Conversation carried on, and conveniently, no one teased me about my choice not to take the flight with a group of women guests here. I wouldn't call myself a player, but I was definitely a flirt. Yet, at the moment I only had one girl in mind: Gemma.

I wasn't prone to focusing on one woman like that, and I had my reasons for it. I didn't want to question it right now though. I was impatient to see Gemma at the grand opening for Cammi's new café tomorrow night. Lately, those of us out here were getting rounded up time and again for the needs of our friends' newest loves. Cammi had the best damned coffee in Alaska, so I was going to support her no matter what.

Of course, the coffee wasn't what had me wound tight with anticipation. That was all Gemma.

Chapter Five

GEMMA

I crossed the parking lot in front of Misty Mountain Café, pausing to spin and look behind me. I was still soaking in every view to be found here. This little coffee shop was situated on a slight hill off of Main Street in Diamond Creek with enough elevation to offer a view of the mountains and a slice of the bay in the distance.

I was still getting accustomed to the long days here. It was June and the sun wouldn't set until after ten p.m. It was evening now, and the sun was only beginning its slide down in the sky. Sunset lasted for hours here in the summer. At the moment, there were the early glimmers of a watercolor sky and the fading brightness of late afternoon.

Turning back, I glanced at the new sign on the café. Cammi must've had that mounted at some point during the day today. I smiled. The renovated Quonset hut was adorable. Windows had been cut into the sides of the structure, and the front, where the door was on the long end of the cylindrical shape, was all windows. Walking inside, I glanced around at the artwork hung on the walls in the already crowded space milling with customers and guests. In addition to her incredible coffee, Cammi had partnered with Daphne for baked goods and updated the sandwich menu.

As I glanced around, a voice came from over my shoulder. "Hey, Gemma!"

Turning, I found Susie Winters smiling at me. Her brown curls bounced and her matching brown eyes crinkled at the corners with her smile. I'd met Susie through Cammi, encountering her occasionally at the coffee shop in the short time I'd been in town. Come to think of it, almost everyone I'd met so far had either been from students coming to my yoga classes, or people I met here.

"Hey, Susie, how's it going?"

"Good, good," she said quickly. "Doesn't it look great?"

"It does, and I love the new sign outside."

Susie's husband, Jared Winters, approached, looping his arm around her waist. "You've met my husband, right?" Susie asked.

"Just once, good to see you again," I responded with a nod to Jared.

"If you haven't been out fishing yet, you need to go," Susie added.

Jared's grin shifted from her to me. "Just let Susie know if you'd like to go, and you can hitch a ride on one of our trips." I knew from Susie that Jared and his two brothers ran a fishing charter business.

"I'll make sure to do that," I replied.

Susie was drawn away into another conversation, so I threaded my way through the crowd to say hello to Cammi who was standing by the counter. "Love the sign," I commented.

"Jessa painted it. She's the one who does the tables too," Cammi explained, gesturing over to a table nearby.

I looked in that direction, seeing a woman with wavy brown hair standing beside yet another handsome man. Alaska was crowded as far as the rugged, handsome man quotient went. Outdoorsy was definitely the vibe.

The tables here were whimsically painted and fun. Cammi explained to me they served as a way to show off Jessa's artwork, which she sold out at one of the galleries near Otter Cove Harbor.

"I need to get out to the galleries one of these days," I commented.

"You should. Would you like coffee or some food? I even have wine and hard cider tonight," Cammi said with a smile. "And it's all on the house."

"I'll take a few of those," I said, pointing to a cluster of pastries on a tray. "A small glass of the cider would be nice too. I'm driving, so I can just have a taste."

One of Cammi's staff poured me a glass and passed over a small plate. Cammi was already swept into another conversation. I was scanning the room to see who else I knew when I heard a voice low at my shoulder. "Hey, Gemma."

A prickle raced down my spine the second I recognized Diego's unmistakable voice—warm with a hint of gruffness. Turning, I found him looking his usual delectable self. His dark hair was slightly rumpled, but then that always seemed to be the case. His green eyes stood out against his sun-kissed skin. The man's chiseled jaw and cut cheekbones were too much.

His eyes searched mine briefly, and I thought I

recognized an answering flare of heat in his gaze. "Hey," I said, a little breathlessly.

"You tasting Delia's cider?" he asked

I peered down at the glass in my hand. Looking back to him, I replied, "Um, I'm not sure."

"It must be hers. Cammi's serving from the brewery tonight, and they only bottle Delia's. You've been up to the Lodge restaurant, right?"

I shook my head and took a swallow of the cider, savoring the fresh apple flavor that slid across my tongue. "I keep meaning to get up there, but I haven't yet."

Diego held my gaze for a long moment. "I'll take you then. The food is excellent, and you can meet Delia. The lodge gives you another pool of customers for your yoga classes. There are plenty of staff between the restaurant and the lodge itself."

"Is it busy during the summer? I thought it was a ski lodge."

Diego held his finger up when a waiter passing by with a tray asked if he wanted anything. He took several of the small finger sandwiches and his own glass of cider before returning his focus to me.

"It's primarily a ski lodge," he explained after a swallow of cider. "During the summer, they run hiking trips and function as a regular hotel. They send us plenty of business for our flight service."

"Aren't they your competition?"

I took a bite of a pastry, closing my eyes and letting out a little moan at the flavor. It was filled with brie and a burst of cranberry flavor. "Oh, my God, that's good."

When I opened my eyes, he was staring at me intently. "You could do that again," he murmured.

While nothing he said was inappropriate, there

was a naughty hint to his words. It felt as if sparks scattered over the surface of my skin. Trying to play it cool, which I was utterly terrible at, I commented, "You should taste one."

He took one, while I enjoyed another. After a moment, he nodded. "Very good. To your question, the ski lodge isn't really competition. They cater to a different type of tourist. Sure, they are Alaskan tourists, but the people that book there want to be close to town. The people that stay with us are more after the pretending as if they're in the middle of nowhere vibe."

I couldn't help but giggle at that description. "Pretending? Aren't you all pretty far out there?"

Diego finished another bite, and I found my eyes lingering on the motion of his throat when he swallowed. Good Lord. I even thought this man swallowing was sexy. This wasn't even sane. Heat prickled over the surface of my skin, and my pulse hummed along.

Oblivious to my internal state, he stayed on topic. "You'll have to come out there. It's only twenty minutes away from town. It does have the feel of being isolated though. More than half the drive is on a gravel road. It's pretty high end and a really nice place. Plus, we have Daphne's cooking. As you can see from her sandwiches, we've got it good."

"Oh, is there a restaurant there?"

Diego chuckled. "No. That would be nice though. It's a restaurant grade kitchen, but we only serve the guests there."

Elias, Cammi's boyfriend, approached. He appeared to hear the tail end of our conversation. "That's the only thing I miss."

Glancing to him, Diego flashed a grin, sending

butterflies into flight in my belly, even though he wasn't grinning at me. "Of course, you do. But you know you miss me more," he teased.

"No, he misses losing to me and cards," Gabriel, another pilot there, offered when he stopped beside us.

The guys lapsed into an easygoing and teasing conversation, and I wondered what it was like to have that kind of friendship. Although, I had friends where I grew up, Portland was a big city, and my struggles in school tended to leave me feeling insecure most of the time. My closest friends were from softball, and we'd all been splintered by what happened with our coach. I still stayed in touch with a few of them, but the tension from that episode lingered. Several of us shared the uneasy bond of being the target of his attention, while others didn't. That dynamic created a strange fracture in our relationships. I hated how the situation continued to ripple through my life.

Nora, another pilot and Flynn's sister who I'd met at yoga classes with Daphne, wandered over and cast a smile. "How is yoga going? I need to come to more classes," she said apologetically.

"I'm actually pretty busy. I'm finding ways to cater to the tourists for the summer."

"Oh, you should give us your flyers. We'll hand them out to our guests. We have a running list of things that we tell them about, so if anyone wants a yoga class, we'll send them to you." Nora's eyes brightened. "Would you do classes out at the resort? Maybe once a week."

I pondered that for a moment. "I could certainly do that. We would need to make sure there's space. Once a week would work."

Just then, Flynn and Daphne meandered over. "Those little pastries you made are incredible," I said.

She flashed a smile in return, smoothing her hand over her auburn hair, which was pulled back in a twist. "I'm glad you like them."

Nora nudged Flynn in the side. "I have an idea. Why don't we pay Gemma to come out and do a yoga class once a week for guests? Maybe one evening a week?"

Flynn glanced to me. "If you think it's worthwhile, it's fine with me."

Daphne clapped her hands together. "I love this idea." She looked between Flynn and Nora. "We should schedule it on one of the nights we don't serve guests dinner. Gemma can stay after and have dinner with us."

"Oh, well, it's a done deal if you're cooking," I interjected.

The night passed quickly, complete with a few prizes given away in a raffle for fishing trips and the like. Nora also convinced me that I needed to go dipnetting for salmon with her. I wasn't sure I completely understood what it was, but she promised me it would be fun and that I could watch since I hadn't been a resident for a full year yet. Although I hadn't been in Alaska too long, I'd quickly discovered there were strict regulations around fishing and hunting and that one wasn't considered a resident until they'd lived here for a full year. Not that I did much of either, but there were signs aplenty warning tourists to be aware of the laws. Nora explained dipnetting was exactly as it sounded—dipping a net in the water to catch salmon.

I was acutely aware of Diego the entire evening. He wasn't always at my side, but my eyes searched him

out again and again and again. It didn't help that he
was so easy on the eyes. My girl parts also thought the
view was excellent, but I managed to keep my cool. I
ended up offering to help Cammi clean up afterwards.

Daphne, Nora, and the guys from the resort also
helped. Daphne effectively bossed all of them around.
The sun was slipping down behind the horizon by the
time I walked out to the parking lot. Cammi called
goodbye from the door, and I waved over my shoulder.
When I got to my small car, I found Diego's truck
parked right beside it.

I even recognized the back of him now. He was
leaning over to put something in the back of his truck,
and I took the moment to admire his muscled ass. The
man had one fine ass. *Every* inch of him was fine. He
straightened and closed his truck cap, turning just as I
stopped near my car and hit the key fob to unlock it.

We didn't speak and simply looked at each other
for a moment. The air felt lit with a charge. "Need
some help," Diego finally asked, a grin teasing at the
corners of his mouth.

Startled, I looked down at the paper plate I held in
my hand. Cammi had given me a few of the leftover
pastries. "I think I can handle it," I managed when I
looked back up into his teasing eyes.

Opening the passenger door, I set the plate on the
seat and placed my purse beside it. When I closed the
door, I pressed my hands against it, as if it could
somehow anchor me while this intense and inconvenient desire for Diego did cartwheels through my
body.

I hadn't noticed that he had walked between our
vehicles and was standing only a foot or so away from
me. My pulse rioted, and butterflies tickled my belly.

There didn't happen to be anyone else in the

parking lot at the moment, and we were shielded by Diego's truck from the view of the coffee shop.

"I wanted to kiss you the other day," he said, his low voice sending a hot shiver over my skin as it prickled with goosebumps.

"You did?" I squeaked.

This was shocking to me, and I didn't know why. I was always surprised to think anyone might want me. The reasons behind that were something I didn't like to ponder.

He nodded slowly. "I'd like to kiss you now."

He stepped a little closer, and air was suddenly hard to come by as my pulse went *absolutely* wild. I could suddenly think of nothing other than kissing him.

"What do you think about that?" The mere sound of his voice sent sparks pinwheeling through me.

I realized he was giving me an out, but also pushing me to tell him what I wanted. And, oh, how I wanted to kiss him!

I took something like a breath, although it wasn't much use with my lungs doing a poor job. "I'd like that," I finally replied in a breathy whisper.

I wasn't a breathy girl. I was practical and logical and carved my own path in life. I didn't get all fluttery over a sexy guy who wanted to kiss me. Except, apparently, I did with Diego.

"Let's test that theory then," he murmured, taking another step until he was right there in front of me, every masculine, muscled inch of him.

Diego's presence was a potent force. I could feel all of him, the power and strength contained inside his strong body. He moved, almost lazily. In a corner of my mind, I marveled at him, thinking he must have way more experience at this than me. It was just a kiss.

And we hadn't even gotten to the kiss yet. The mere anticipation of it had me feeling as if I were leaning on the edge of something, about to topple over. He lifted his hand, his thumb tracing along my jaw and then around my lips. His eyes searched mine as my insides turned molten.

He said something, but my brain couldn't absorb it, right before dipping his head and brushing his lips across mine. That subtle touch was like lightning in my body, sizzling hot and sending fire licking through my veins.

My breath was followed by a shameless moan escaping from my lips. He brushed his lips over mine once more, sending another bolt of lightning through my system. My brain cells scattered, and I curled my arms around his shoulders, flexing into him just as his hand slid around to cup my nape. He angled my head and took command of our kiss.

I felt the heated path of his palm slide down the center of my spine, coming to rest above my bottom, his fingers splaying. He emitted a soft growl right before his tongue swept into my mouth.

Diego obliterated all memories of prior kisses. His mouth was deliciously teasing as his tongue glided against mine before he drew back and dropped kisses on each corner of my lips. I was already in danger of melting as rapidly as ice under hot sunlight. When he did that, I whimpered, my fingers digging into the corded muscles along his spine as I pressed closer.

Along with that fiery heat dancing through my veins, there was a tug low in my belly, and my pulse thundered through my body. He played with my mouth with lazy teases of his tongue and lingering kisses.

I could hardly believe it as I plastered myself

against him, my nipples tight and achy, and wet heat slick between my thighs. His lips blazed a path away from my mouth, pressing hot, open kisses along the underside of my jaw, his teeth grazing the side of my neck.

"Diego," I pleaded, rocking my hips restlessly against him.

The sound of a car door in the distance punctured the haze of fierce need clouding my mind. Diego lifted his head, but he didn't step away, keeping me held in a full body clench against him.

Sweet hell. I wanted to stay in this singular spot in the universe for the rest of my life, held tight against his strong body.

Chapter Six

DIEGO

Gemma stared up at me, her eyes glazed, her cheeks pink, and her lips kiss-swollen. Meanwhile, every beat of my heart was like flint against stone and sent sparks flying through me.

I was almost shaken. I had control, but just barely. It had been over five years since any girl got to me like this. I thought it wasn't even possible anymore. That I'd been burned enough that it left skid marks on my heart as a reminder of what not to do.

I knew I wanted Gemma, but with desire there was never a guarantee emotion would tangle inside of it. With her, a rush of emotion and a sense of protectiveness twined like vines within my need for her.

I managed to breathe, and another car door slammed nearby. It took all the discipline I had to ease my hold on Gemma's sweet curves and take a step back.

If anyone happened to walk by our vehicles now, they would see us standing at a respectable distance apart. A gust of wind blew, sending a loose curl across her cheek. Without thinking, I lifted my hand and brushed it away from her eyes, tucking it behind her ear. I almost kissed her again when she bit her lip, and I felt the subtle tremor run through her.

"It sounds like I might see you for a yoga class at the resort. Maybe I could take you to dinner at the lodge soon," I commented.

She licked her lips, and my already aching cock suffered through another jolt of fiery pressure.

"Maybe?" There was a lilt in her voice at the end of the word.

"Let me clarify. Let me take you to dinner there. Just for the food."

Gemma's cheeks flushed a deeper shade of pink, and she let out a husky laugh. "Just the food? I might hold you to that."

"Well now, I'm not promising only the food. Maybe another kiss."

At that moment, the sound of footsteps crossing the gravel parking lot carried to us. Reaching around Gemma, I pushed the passenger door closed because she hadn't shut it completely earlier. At the sound of the click, I said, "I'll wait until you go. Text me your choice: a plane ride, or dinner."

Gemma bit her lip and nodded quickly before hurrying around her car to climb in. I watched when she drove away and waved good night to Elias and Cammi who were locking up the coffee shop.

———

One week later

"Dude, I can't believe you don't have a whole passel of kids," Flynn commented as he leaned back in his chair at the table in the main kitchen at the resort.

It was staff night only, and we were all lounging around the table. Flynn's comment came on the heels of a speaker phone call with my twin nieces who needed help with math homework. I was pretty good at math, but I'd enlisted some group assistance with one of the algebra equations.

I shrugged. "Not yet. We'll see if it ever happens."

Once upon a time, I'd wanted to tie the knot and have kids fast. Young love was stupid sometimes.

"You were engaged before, right?" Gabriel chimed in.

I nodded slowly. "Oh, yeah. I was engaged the first year I was in the Air Force. I was supposed to go home and get married that summer. That's not how it worked out."

Tucker's sharp gaze lifted to mine. "You were fucking cranky as hell when you came back, but you never did tell us what happened. Want to fill us in?"

These guys were my best friends, and for the most part they weren't too nosy. I couldn't even hold it against them if they had questions because I sure as hell didn't shy away from offering my opinion on their private lives.

I lifted my pint glass of beer and took a long swallow. Setting it down, I replied, "I learned that I was too young and didn't know any better yet."

"Man, you're always telling us how in love your parents were. I don't see you just dumping some girl because you decided you were too young. That's not how being young and stupid works," Gabriel commented.

"It wasn't that simple. She was the accountant for my father's business and one of my sister's best friends in college. That's how we knew each other. She was a good enough accountant that she knew how to steal from my parents' business and cover her tracks, at least for a year. That was a deal breaker for me. It would've sat better if she tried to steal my money rather than my parents."

Flynn looked suitably horrified, his brows flying up. "Fuck. That's bullshit."

"Exactly. Don't worry, she didn't break my heart too bad. Like I said, we were young. It burned, but there was no way we were going to be able to work things out after that."

Cat came in from the main room, her ponytail bouncing as she approached the table.

"Looks like you're about to ask Flynn something," I said with a grin.

Cat narrowed her eyes at me. "Don't ruin it for me."

Flynn glanced up. "What is it?"

"Can I spend the night at Shannon's house?"

Flynn's eyes flicked up to the clock mounted on the wall above the doorway. "How are you going to get there?"

"Nora said she's going to town. She can bring me," Cat replied swiftly.

Flynn nodded. "All right, then. I'll call her mom and confirm. How you gonna get home tomorrow?"

Cat let out an aggrieved sigh. "I figured somebody would be going out to fly tomorrow and could pick me up. Wouldn't want to put you out," she said sarcastically.

That rolled off Flynn's shoulders easy. He chuckled. "Of course, somebody will be flying. I'd be happy to pick you up, but I didn't know if you already had a plan."

Cat rolled her eyes and smiled before leaning over

to kiss her older brother's cheek. Nora came in from the back hallway at that moment, and Cat called over, "Flynn said yes. I'll go get my bag."

Nora stopped beside the table, and Elias added, "Cat can hitch a ride with me."

"I was already going," Nora replied. "Just need to see some live music and relax."

Flynn was distracted by something Daphne was saying, but I didn't miss Gabriel standing and commenting, "I might go with you if you don't mind."

"Of course not," Nora said quickly. Her cheeks flushed pink, and I wondered when those two we're going to stop trying to sneak around.

That answer remained firmly in the column of topics that were none of my damn business. At least, according to Gabriel. One time, only once, Tucker teased him about it, and I'd chimed in as well. Gabriel got all pissy and denied it six ways to Sunday.

Our dinner group gradually filtered apart. We were back at the other house when my cell phone buzzed in my pocket. Sliding it out, I smiled the moment I saw *Hot Yoga Teacher* on the banner.

Hot Yoga Teacher: *What about both?*

Diego: *A plane ride and dinner?*

Hot Yoga Teacher: *Yes, please.*

Diego: *You got it, sugar. Tell me what day works for you?*

Hot Yoga Teacher: *What day works for you? You'll be the one flying me. I only teach yoga Monday through Friday.*

Diego: *Sunday?*

I knew my Sunday was open, and that was the one day we never had any delivery trips unless there was a random emergency. That meant there would definitely be a plane available.

Hot Yoga Teacher: *Sunday is perfect.*

Diego: *I'll text you the time.*

Chapter Seven

GEMMA

"Oh, wow," I breathed as I peered out the window of the small plane.

Diego had given me a set of headphones, so we could talk easily over the sound of the engine. I could still hear the rumble of it, but we didn't have to shout over the noise.

"Incredible, right?" came his reply.

"Definitely."

Kachemak Bay stretched out to one side under the plane as Diego hugged the shoreline on the far side of the bay across from Diamond Creek. Lush evergreen trees filled the lower flanks of the mountains, giving way to rocks and a glacier that glowed an otherworldly blue under the sunshine. We'd seen a grizzly bear grazing in an open field only moments ago. Diego was confident the bear was enjoying some berries, although we weren't low enough for him to say what kind. We'd also seen several moose chewing on alder trees, and even a sea lion swimming in the shallows of the water, its form massive and blurry under the water.

"It feels like I could reach out and touch the mountains," I commented.

"I think that every time I fly here," he replied with a chuckle.

He'd filled me in on his job—scenic trips for tourists interspersed with deliveries of groceries and mail to several towns and villages scattered along the shores. Sometimes they flew far enough North that they needed to stop and refuel on the way back. They also took trips over to the famed Katmai National Park for the world-famous viewing of the massive brown bears who caught salmon in the river. I was all set with seeing bears from a distance. It had been enough of a shocker to see the ones mounted in the airport, standing over twelve feet tall. It looked as if humans would be nothing more than a plaything if they swatted them with their giant paws and those long claws.

"Going to head back now. Sound good?"

I experienced a full body shiver at the sound of Diego's voice right in my ears. There was something so intimate about it.

"Sounds good." Aside from the view, I enjoyed watching him maneuver the plane with ease and confidence.

When he glanced to the side at my reply and his eyes caught mine, heat chased like a scatter of hot sparks over my skin. With nothing more than a glance, the intensity contained in his gaze set my nerves alight.

Chapter Eight

DIEGO

Gemma took a bite of halibut and let out a moan as she swallowed. "Oh, my God," she said when she finished chewing. "That's incredible."

I knew she was commenting on the food, obviously, but I was focused on the sight of her tongue darting out to catch a drop of sauce on the corner of her mouth and thinking I shouldn't be so turned on by watching her eat.

"I don't think I've had that yet," I replied, managing to drag my brain back to the topic at hand.

"You have to have a bite," she insisted.

She pushed her plate closer, so I took a bite. The halibut was flaky, but also rich with a creamy texture. It had been drizzled with some kind of a lemon dill sauce.

"Absolutely delicious," I offered.

"I see why this place is so busy." She glanced around the restaurant, taking in the crowded space. Every table was full, but the space didn't feel crowded.

The lodge was originally only open in the winter for skiing. The Hamilton family, who owned the place, had expanded the business since they brought it back to life after years of being closed. They offered hiking, biking, and coordinated with a number of other local tourist services, including Flynn's flight business, to keep their guests happy.

This restaurant occupied the main building of the lodge. It had views of the ski slopes and mountains immediately surrounding it, along with a beautiful view of a slice of Kachemak Bay in the distance. The large room had a tall ceiling with beams crisscrossing the space. It had a modern, yet woodsy feel to it.

Delia Hamilton came out of the swinging doors from the kitchen into the restaurant, checking in at a few tables and then stopping beside ours. "How is it?" she asked, looking between Gemma and me.

"Always amazing," I replied quickly.

Her blue eyes swung to Gemma expectantly. "Delicious," Gemma replied firmly.

"Excellent. Do you need anything?"

"Not at all," I replied as Gemma shook her head.

"I'm planning to get to one of your yoga classes soon," Delia offered. "I'm on my feet all the time, so I'm hoping it'll help me loosen up my back."

"I'll be glad to have you," Gemma replied with a smile. "This place is really nice."

"Delia is the chef and runs the restaurant. Her husband, Garrett, owns this place with his brothers and sisters. He's a lawyer, so I try to stay on his good side," I quipped.

Delia chuckled. "He is, but he's not vicious. These days, he's traded his corporate career for things like fishing and hunting issues and property disputes. He loves it."

"I imagine there's no shortage of interesting cases here in Alaska," Gemma commented.

"There is certainly plenty of variety," Delia added. "I need to run check on things up front. Nice to meet you Gemma, and I'll definitely come by one of your classes soon."

Delia hurried off, her honey blond hair swinging in a ponytail as she crossed the restaurant and disappeared through the archway into the reception area.

We settled in to enjoy our dinners, with a few interruptions, including one from Gage Hamilton, who'd resurrected the ski lodge. Or, so I'd been told by Nora, who kept all of us up to speed on all the local gossip, seeing as she'd grown up here.

"Good to meet you," Gage said with a quick smile toward Gemma before he disappeared into the kitchen.

"Is there anyone you don't know?" Gemma asked as she pushed her plate away and dabbed at the corners of her mouth with her napkin.

"There are plenty of people I don't know," I replied with a chuckle. "I've lived here for five years though. If you stick around, you'll discover it's hard not to get to know all the locals. Tourist season is another ball game. We know these guys well because we send people to them, and they send people to us. It's a two-way street. That's mostly how I've gotten to know people here. You'll see, it'll happen for you. Are you planning to stay?"

Gemma's eyes held mine for a moment. I thought I saw uncertainty passing like shadows through her gaze, but she lifted her chin and nodded. "That's the plan. I just need to make sure I can make it work financially."

"Your classes are always full when I'm there."

Her lips quirked with a smile. "That's because Daphne corrals all of you guys there. She's been great for my business. Classes are full, and that's a good thing."

"What brought you to Alaska?" I asked.

Alaska was filled with transplants. It was sparsely populated for many years and still was. Everyone had a story for the how and why behind what brought them here. Whether it was for a change of pace, or because they wanted to experience this kind of wilderness. We all had a reason.

Gemma's eyes cast down for a moment, and she took the last swallow of her wine. Her shoulders rose and fell with a breath, and I sensed trepidation from her. Even though I didn't know the story, protectiveness rose inside me. We had only shared a kiss. Mind you, that kiss stood the test as one of the hottest kisses of my life. I'd only known her for a matter of months, and yet here I was, wanting to protect her from whatever I saw flickering in her eyes.

"I needed a change. I wasn't sure where I was going to find that change, but I actually won a trip here. Not to Diamond Creek, but to Anchorage. I loved it, but I didn't really want to do the city thing and Anchorage is an actual city. A woman at the place where I was staying, suggested I check out Diamond Creek. I did, and I came across the job to take care of the horses. Since it came with the house, I took it as a sign because I love horses and riding. That job covers my bills, so I figured it was the perfect way to get started here. What brought you here?"

"Air Force," I said simply.

"Were you stationed in Alaska?"

I shook my head. "I was in the Air Force with Flynn, Elias, Gabriel, and Tucker. Flynn came back to take care of his brother and two sisters after their mother passed away. He invited the rest of us to come work for him whenever we left the Air Force because he needed pilots. Elias and I came up around the same time, about five years ago. Tucker and Gabriel made it another year later."

"You guys seem pretty tight."

"We are, they're like family to me."

"Where are you originally from?" she asked.

"I was a military brat. My father was in the Air Force too. We lived all over. I have four sisters, but both of our parents have passed away."

"I'm sorry to hear that," she said quickly.

"Thank you. It's been a few years, and I still miss them. I was blessed. They loved each other and loved us, so we're all still tight even though none of us live in the same place. What about you? Where are you from?"

"Portland, Oregon. My parents and my brother still live there."

"What does your family think of you coming up to Alaska?"

"They're supportive, but they'd like me closer to home. I keep reminding them there are actually direct flights from Portland here, and it's not that far."

I sensed Gemma was uncomfortable talking about her family, so I let it drop, commenting casually, "Most families wish everyone would stay in the same place."

After the waiter came to clear our plates and checked on dessert, Gemma passed. I almost ordered a dessert, but she caught my eyes. "I have brownies at my house."

"Does that mean I can have one?" I teased, loving how her cheeks pinkened.

Her teeth dented her bottom lip, sending a sizzle of lust through me, before she nodded. "Of course, you can have one."

I asked the waiter to bring the check. When he left, promising to return with it, Gemma said, "We're splitting the check."

I looked over at her. "I invited you to dinner, so I'm covering it."

Her lips pressed in a line. "No, we're splitting it."

"How about you invite me to dinner and you can return the favor?" I countered.

Gemma's eyes glinted as she looked over at me. She let out a throaty chuckle, which sent a shot of lust straight through me. "Fine. Next time, I'll cover it."

On the way out, I couldn't resist resting my hand on her back, right at the dip of her waist, just above the sweet curve of her bottom. Only the fact that we were out in public kept me from sliding my palm over that curve. I knew how it felt, and I greedily wanted that sensation again. I wasn't sure what I was doing with Gemma, but I was certain I wanted her. With a fierceness that surprised me.

When we'd texted about today, I told her I needed to pick her up because there wasn't much parking at the plane hangar. Which was true, but not really.

I'd wanted her to myself. Even more than that, I'd wanted her on my motorcycle again, this time not chasing after a horse.

We got out to my bike again, and I handed her the helmet. "Do you always keep an extra helmet?"

I shook my head. "Nope, just for you."

Her eyes widened slightly, but she didn't say anything further. She climbed on behind me. I savored the feel of her curves pressing against my back as she looped her arms around my waist.

In general, I didn't take people for rides on my bike, much less women. I always had an extra helmet at the house, because I had sisters. Cat had once badgered me into taking her for a short ride. Much to my dismay, Flynn had agreed when I told her she had to ask him. She was like a little sister to me, and I didn't want to worry about her safety any more than I wanted to worry about my own sisters' safety.

By the time I rolled up to a stop at Gemma's place, I was thinking I needed to turn around on the bike and have my way with her right then and there. But, I didn't. I had some manners, after all.

Chapter Nine

GEMMA

My body was humming with the vibration of Diego's motorcycle when he cut the engine. I took a breath and reluctantly loosened my arms from around his waist. Tonight's ride was different from the first one. Then, I'd been startled at Diego's appearance and unsettled with Charlie running loose. Tonight, I knew what it felt like to be held by him and loved the feel of his muscled body against mine.

Just when I was thinking it might be nice if he spun around and had his way with me on his motorcycle, I heard the sound of hoofbeats and glanced toward the pasture to see Charlie cantering over with two other horses right behind him. There were four horses here, but the oldest one tended to linger by the paddock. Shasta was the friendliest horse of the group, but due to his age he tended to be stiff. I babied him with treats on the regular.

Diego swung his leg over, removing his helmet as he stood beside the motorcycle. I climbed off behind him and handed him the helmet, smoothing my hand over my hair. "Gorgeous night for a ride," I commented.

It was approaching nine at night, and the sky was just now fading from light to dark. It was that magical twilight time where the stars twinkled in the silvery light of dusk and the fading colors from the sunset lingered.

Diego nodded, his eyes arcing across the pasture toward the view of the mountains and the water in the distance. "The horses are happy to see you," he said with a slow grin when his eyes landed on mine again.

What he said was benign, but the look contained in his gaze set butterflies alight in my belly and my pulse racing as heat spun through me.

"They're curious. Don't worry, they're not hungry. I fed them before you picked me up."

"Do they stay in the pasture all night?"

I shook my head. "I need to put them in their stalls. Want to help?"

"Of course." He tucked the spare helmet into the compartment under the seat and set his on top of the seat before falling into step beside me.

My senses were heightened, attuned to the frequency of Diego's presence. The sound of our footsteps on the gravel was broken by an owl calling in the trees nearby. When the horses saw me heading toward the barn with Diego, they trotted over to meet us there.

Stepping through the large sliding door into the barn, the soothing scents struck me—hay, horses, and an underlying hint of leather. These were the smells of my childhood when I rode horses. My mother had ridden horses, and we had neighbors who had a farm where we rode nearby. It was a calming spot in my childhood where it always felt like I was scrambling to catch up to the brilliance of my parents and my brother.

Dyslexia was a common learning disability, but it was still confusing when nobody knew what was going on. Sadly, my parents' high expectations for my brilliance had interfered with the school figuring out the issue sooner. Once doubt seeps into your soul, it lingers, like mold that you can't get out of a room sometimes. I'd largely come to peace with that. I knew my parents loved me, but what happened had shaped my childhood. School is such a big part of childhood that when it's not going well and you're struggling, it could turn into a bundle of uncertainty and insecurity. Horses and softball were what I'd loved during those years, and only one of those loves remained unscathed.

Diego glanced around. "Nice barn."

It was a small barn and well-maintained. There were four stalls with an aisle in between. Crossing to the other end of the barn, I opened the door to the small paddock. My elderly buddy, Shasta, walked slowly into the barn, lifting his nose to nudge me in the shoulder.

"Hey, sweetie," I said, scratching him on the forehead. He turned his attention to Diego, curiously sniffing him and nibbling lightly on his shoulder as he passed by.

"I think that's his version of a kiss," I said with a laugh.

Diego didn't seem bothered in the slightest, instantly endearing himself to me. He laughed as he greeted Shasta. Shasta had once been a speckled horse, as I knew from the photographs in the house, but he was almost all white now. He enjoyed being brushed, so I groomed him daily and took care of his mane and tail, which he flicked affectionately when he passed by. Shasta knew the routine well and walked into his stall, the closest one by the door to the paddock.

Charlie came trotting through, stopping quickly to greet Diego and appearing to recognize him. "I think he knows he's seen me before," Diego said with a chuckle.

"Probably. It was memorable, what with the motorcycle and all."

After Charlie went into his stall, the other two horses followed. One was a dark bay with a star on his forehead, owned by a woman who lived down the road and came by fairly regularly. The other was a chestnut with a wide white blaze on his face. He was also owned by a neighbor nearby, although his owner didn't stop by as often.

Once all the horses were in their stalls, Diego followed my lead without me needing to explain it, closing and latching their stall doors. We fetched some hay, and he helped me toss it into their stalls.

As we walked out, my belly shimmied with nervous anticipation. I wanted to invite him inside, but I couldn't remember the last time I had invited anyone into a place where I lived.

Apparently, my mouth was ahead of my brain, and my question tumbled out. "Would you like to come in?"

"Of course. Don't you remember? You promised me the perfect brownie."

"Oh, right. Did I say the brownies were perfect?"

"Maybe not exactly, but that's why we passed on dessert. Now, if you've changed your mind, I won't insist."

When I glanced sideways and saw his teasing smile, my belly did a few flips and butterflies spun like mad. "Oh, I insist," I managed, feeling my cheeks heat.

The place I was renting was a small, ranch-style home. We went in through the front door, which was in the center of the rectangular-shaped structure and had a small curved porch. It opened into the living room. To one side was an archway that led into the kitchen and dining room area, and the other archway on the other end led into a hallway with three bedrooms and a bathroom. Like everywhere in Alaska, or so it seemed, the house had a view through the trees with a glimpse of the mountains to the side.

Diego glanced around. "Nice place."

"I love it," I said. "It came furnished and everything."

I kicked off my shoes by the door, and he followed suit. "Follow me." I gestured as I began to cross through the archway to the kitchen. "I'll get that brownie for you."

Chocolate was one of my favorite things, and I made incredible brownies, if I did say so myself. They were decadent with melted dark chocolate in the center. Heated, with vanilla ice cream, it was about the best simple dessert in the universe as far as I was concerned.

Diego followed me in, taking in the kitchen. It had counters lining three walls with a small oval table by the windows in what served as a casual dining area.

"Have a seat," I called over my shoulder. "Do you want anything to drink with dessert?"

"Just water will do."

I quickly sliced two brownies and heated them in the microwave. Only moments later, I was sitting across from Diego, watching as he took a bite and let out a rough moan. The sound vibrated through me. It seemed everything he did spoke to my hormones. They sent up a little cheer of approval.

"Damn. That's fucking amazing," he said flatly. "It really is the best brownie I've ever had."

I didn't know why I was blushing over brownies, but here I was.

"I'm glad to hear it. I'm sure Delia has desserts just as good as this. Everything else there is five-star quality."

Diego took another bite. "Agreed that everything she makes is excellent, but I'm not sure she can beat this brownie. With the ice cream, it might be the food version of God."

I laughed and took a bite.

"So, what did you think of the plane ride?" he asked a few moments later after he set his spoon down and pushed his empty bowl away.

"It was awesome. I've never been in a small plane like that. I kind of can't believe that's your job."

He grinned. "Sometimes I can't believe it either. I've been flying for years. That's why I went into the Air Force. I wanted to fly planes. I didn't know I'd luck into a job like this after I got out of the military."

"I bet you guys love it."

"We do. I have a job I love, and I get to work with people who are family to me. Can't really beat it. I'm a happy man."

A fierce sense of longing pierced me. That feeling, what he described, was what I wanted—feeling like I had my place in the world and I had my own little tribe. That was something I felt like I'd been searching for forever.

Restless, I stood to put our bowls in the sink. I felt him stand and cross over into the kitchen behind me. His presence was potent, all raw, primal, and easy masculinity. It wasn't overpowering, but so complete.

Turning, I found him leaning against the counter, one hand curled on the edge and the other hooked in a pocket. There was nothing left to do just now, and anxiety spun inside me.

"Come'ere," he murmured, his voice gruff.

Since apparently I did whatever Diego asked, I crossed the kitchen to stop in front of him. He reached a hand out, catching one of mine and reeling me closer to him. The heat emanating from him buffeted my body, and desire flickered to life, sending flames licking through me.

"I'm going to kiss you again," he said slowly and with purpose, each word like a drop of liquid fire spinning into the need building inside me.

I licked my lips, and tried to take a breath. "Okay," I whispered.

Then, his hand was sliding around my waist and pulling me flush against him. I felt his breath like a soft breeze on my skin as he dipped his head and dusted a kiss on my neck right behind my ear, sending a hot shiver through me. He made his way to my mouth at a leisurely pace, pressing hot, open kisses on the underside of my jaw. He dropped kisses at each corner of my mouth before he finally, *finally*, fit his mouth over mine.

That couldn't have taken more than a few seconds, and yet the moment was so fraught with tension and need that by the time his tongue swept into my mouth, I was near frantic. I moaned shamelessly into our kiss, my tongue greedy against his. He growled in response, his hand sliding down to cup my bottom. I felt the hard, hot press of his arousal at the apex of my thighs. I wanted all of him. *Now*.

He devoured my mouth with masterful strokes, easing back only to nip at my lips and dive back in. I was greedy, one hand mapping his chest and the other stealing under his shirt. My God, he was *all* muscle. His skin was warm to the touch and felt alive as I stroked my palm across it.

He muttered something, tearing his lips free and taking in a ragged breath. I gulped lungfuls of air as my heartbeat thundered and blood rushed through my ears.

His eyes swept over my face. We were quiet, just staring at each other. The moment felt sharply intimate. I'd never felt such the center of anyone's focus. This moment was all there was.

His palm slid away from where he'd been caressing the curve of my bottom. I instantly missed his touch, but then, he lifted his hand, his fingers trailing over my skin along the edge of my blouse. His light touch was a blaze of fire. He paused when his fingertip landed at the center, above the top button.

"Please," I heard myself say, barely even recognizing the throaty, almost pleading quality to my voice. I wasn't a girl who lost herself to passion. This was almost like witnessing a stranger inhabiting a part of myself I'd never known.

Because, apparently, Diego could read my mind, he flicked that top button open and worked his way down —one tantalizing button at a time.

Chapter Ten

DIEGO

Gemma's blouse had these maddening tiny buttons. I'd never thought a button would have anything to do with the state of my body, but the tension created by them as I undid them one at a time felt like a coil tightening inside me. Matters were made decidedly worse by her breathy whimpers and the feel of her palm mapping across my chest.

When her shirt fell open, and I glimpsed her dark blue lace bra, heat sizzled up my spine, and I let out a rough groan. She was pressed against me, so I spun us around quickly, lifting her and sliding her hips on the counter. She let out a surprised gasp, and I felt a grin kicking up the corners of my mouth when I looked at her.

"Sorry to startle you there, sugar," I murmured before stringing a trail of kisses along her collarbone.

I tortured myself a little, sliding my palm over the soft curve of her belly before coasting up to cup one of her breasts. It fit perfectly in my palm, a lush weight. I stroked my thumb over the lace, feeling her nipple pebble under my touch. Her eyes were heavy-lidded, and her breath came in sharp, rapid pants.

I needed her mouth again and closed the short distance between us to capture her plump, damp lips. She kissed like a dream, her mouth opening immediately, hot and sweet. Her tongue was sassy with mine, and she tasted a bit like chocolate, a special kind of heaven I hadn't imagined. Chocolate and kisses went incredibly well together.

I took sip after languid sip of her mouth, all the while getting to know the feel of her body under my hands. I slid one hand around her waist over the silky skin, my fingers sliding just under the waist of her jeans to cup her bottom. I was relieved they weren't too tight because I was all about easy access at the moment.

Everything about Gemma was soft and warm and sensual. Meanwhile, my cock was hard as a steel rod and aching for her. I wanted her, badly, but this was just for her tonight. Although I never was one to shy away from a hot encounter where everyone got what they wanted, I was somehow holding back with Gemma. Like I knew it would be all the better for me if I waited.

I finally broke free from her delectable mouth, murmuring, "You taste so fucking good."

She replied with something between a moan and a whimper as I squeezed a nipple between my thumb and forefinger just before I undid the clasp between her breasts. Straightening, I let my eyes dip down. Her breasts tumbled loose, plump and round, with her nipples deep pink, both taut peaks practically begging for my mouth.

Whether they were begging or not, I needed to taste them and dipped my head, catching one nipple with my lips. I gave it a slow swirl with my tongue and a light suck before drawing back. I was in danger of coming in my jeans like an untried boy without her even touching me when she let out a ragged cry and gasped my name. I couldn't resist and had to give the same attention to her other breast. I didn't want any part of her body to feel left out.

Gemma reached between us, her palm boldly stroking over my cock. Fuck me. This girl was going to push me to the limits of my discipline. Lifting my head, I thumbed her nipple, savoring the way she arched into my touch.

When she stroked over me again, I murmured, "Easy there."

Her lashes lifted, and her dark, hazy gaze struck me like a whip, spurring my need harder and faster.

"I need—" she began just as I slid my hand over her belly to cup her mound.

Even through the denim, I could feel her heat. "Tell me what you need, sugar."

"Something," she gasped, her tone almost annoyed.

I quickly unbuttoned her jeans and slid her zipper down, that subtle sound spinning into all the other sensations roaming through my body. There was just enough room for me to get my hand in her jeans and discover her panties were wet with her arousal.

I wasn't all about finesse, not tonight. I felt as if I were a rock tumbling down the hill in an avalanche, bouncing wildly as I sought the only thing I wanted. Well, not the *only* thing, but the sole thing I was going to let myself have tonight—her pleasure.

Her hips bucked restlessly into my touch. Although the space was tight, I pushed her panties to the side, delving my fingers in her folds. They were slick with her need. Leaning forward, I caught her lips in mine again, right as she let out a little whimper that I caught in our kiss as I sank one finger and then another, knuckle deep, into her snug core.

Fuck me. The feel of her channel, hot and slick around my touch as I teased her higher and higher, was like nothing I'd ever experienced. I could feel her breasts brush against my chest with her tattered breathing. Even though my T-shirt separated us, the sensation was intoxicating. I clung to my control, delving my tongue inside her mouth and mimicking the motion of my fingers in her channel as she rocked against me.

I could feel her tightening as she rippled around me. I lifted my head because I needed to see this. Her skin was flushed and her lips were pink and swollen. "I want to see your eyes," I said, my voice strained, like the need strung tight inside my body.

Her lashes lifted, her gaze locking to mine instantly. I watched when she flew apart, her eyes closing again as her entire body trembled and she arched, the muscles in her neck tightening with her keening cry.

Chapter Eleven

GEMMA

I barely registered when Diego slowly withdrew his hand and put my panties back in place before zipping my jeans and even buttoning them with one hand. All the while, he held me close. My head fell against his shoulder as I tried to catch my breath after the one and only orgasm I'd ever had with anyone other than myself.

I'd had plenty of sex, just none of it all that great. My experiences with sex were kind of, well, boring. I had actually given up thinking it might ever be much more. Now Diego had gone and completely blown my mind and left me all but a melted puddle in his arms. I felt boneless with sensations flowing through my body like the tide eddying after a crashing wave.

I could feel the hard press of his arousal, just on the inside of my thigh where my legs dangled off the edge of the counter.

I didn't know why, but I sensed he had no intention of taking things further tonight. A small corner of my mind worried about that. My past experience had led me to believe it was a girl's job to make sure

no man was left wanting. I wanted to give Diego
even a spoonful of the pleasure he'd just given me.
Preferably much more. None of this felt dutiful,
which was strangely fraught for me. If only because
of the contrast to past experience. I felt comfortable
in my skin with him in a way I'd never felt with
a man.

I finally found enough strength to lift my head and
open my eyes. I discovered I had one palm curled
around his waist, pressing against the corded muscles
of his spine. I'd orgasmed so hard I hadn't even
noticed part of my body was still clenching his.

His eyes opened, his gaze searching mine. He
dipped his head, giving me a lingering kiss, just enough
to rev the engine of my body all over again, sending
pinwheels of sensation through me and those eddies
stirring into another rush of pleasure.

When he drew away, my question slipped out.
"What about you?"

"Not tonight, sugar," he said in that low, gravelly
voice.

All he had to do was speak and another shiver
chased over the surface of my skin. It felt as if my
libido was coming awake after hibernation, energized
and starved for sustenance.

I surprised myself with another question. "How
come?"

Diego was quiet, and for a second my vulnerability
rose to the surface swiftly. I thought I saw a flicker of
the same in his eyes. It disappeared quickly like the
wing of a bird out of the corner of my eye.

"Because I don't want to rush. Not with you." He
punctuated that with another lingering kiss.

Every touch felt like drops of honey rolling over
my skin, warm and sweet.

"That okay?" he asked, searching my eyes when he lifted his head again.

I was nodding before I thought about it. Because it was okay. Maybe, just maybe, sex didn't have to feel like a transaction. That was a novel thought for me.

He stepped away, helping me off the counter. I pulled my bra closed, and he buttoned my blouse. His knuckles kept brushing against my skin, sparks flying in the wake of every touch.

I felt liquid inside, with little pings of pleasure echoing through my system here and there.

"Today was really awesome," I said as I looked up at him.

His lips curled in a slow smile, and my heart gave a sweet twist in my chest, yet another surprise.

"It *was* really awesome. You owe me dinner, you better not forget."

"I won't. When would you like to go?"

I silently cursed myself for speaking so quickly. I didn't really know the rules of dating. Well, I sort of did. I was terrible at them. Either I wasn't interested, or I didn't do casual well, or I didn't feel a thing, or apparently, I was too eager like this. I think this was against all of the rules. I was supposed to wait before I pushed to see him again, maybe even a prescribed amount of time. I was quite certain I could search online after he left and find any thousands of articles or online discussions about how long to wait and why it was best to wait and why it was important not to seem too eager, and so on and so forth.

As my mind spun its wheels, Diego pulled his phone out of his pocket and tapped on the screen. "I'm scheduled for flights for the next seven days straight." He cast me a regretful look.

My insecure heart cheered at that. He was disappointed. Maybe I hadn't completely blown it by behaving like an enthusiastic puppy.

"How about you let me know then?" I suggested.

"I will. My sister is coming to visit soon too. I don't know exactly when. I promise we'll have dinner soon, but you don't want to have it with her, not right away." He rolled his eyes at that. "She's nosy and might scare you off. I love her though."

I bit my lip, almost laughing at the sweetness in the way he described his sister and the affectionate annoyance in his tone.

"Let's say the next Saturday after my last flight. We always get two days off after we do seven days in a row. I'm guaranteed not to be flying that day."

"What about your sister?"

"If she's here, she'll deal," he returned with a shrug.

Chapter Twelve

DIEGO

A few days later

I drained my coffee and leaned back in my chair at the table in the resort's kitchen. "Damn, that is some good coffee."

Elias chuckled from where he sat across from me at the table. He'd shown up this morning to have a staff-only brunch with us with coffees for everyone from Cammi. She even packed them in an insulated container so they were still warm when he got here.

"Yeah, dude, you can never break up with her," Tucker commented from beside me.

"Definitely not. Needs to be a group vote," Gabriel added.

"I'm not going to break up with her," Elias said. "But that's not because her coffee is amazing."

"We know you're whipped, no need to remind us," Gabriel replied, sounding the slightest bit irritated about this, likely because he didn't get enough since he and Nora were still sneaking around.

Speaking of, Nora came in through the door from the back hallway. She had her own cabin nearby and didn't stay in the family rooms here at the lodge.

"Morning," Nora called as she crossed over to see what Daphne was working on at the stove.

Daphne called to her, "There are omelets in the warming pan, veggie or meat."

Nora smiled as she served herself. Although the resort was busier since Daphne had started working here, she kept a schedule where we had at least one staff-only dinner a week, and one brunch. She insisted it was important for her to get a break from cooking for guests. She said it was also a way to make sure the guests were taking advantage of restaurants in town. Daphne was our chef, but she was also really the manager of the resort these days. Flynn had been so focused on getting the flight service going that everything else here had been a scramble for him.

Daphne had now organized referral flows with practically every other tourist business in town. It was awesome. It gave us a chance to chill out and relax together when guests weren't around.

Nora joined us at the table, slipping into the empty chair beside Gabriel. "So, what's up this morning?" she asked the table at large.

Elias silently slid a coffee cup labeled with her name across the counter. "I think it's still warm. From Cammi."

Nora's eyes went wide. "Oh, man. She's the best. You can't break up with her."

"Jesus Christ." Elias leaned back in his chair. 'What's with this? I have no intention of breaking up with Cammi."

Flynn chuckled at Nora's puzzled look. "We just reminded him he couldn't do that."

Nora grinned, her cheeks dimpling. "Well, we're used to getting coffee at least once a week from her personally delivered by you. Plus, we don't want it to be awkward at the two best coffee shops in town."

Conversation meandered along. Daphne, because she was all business even when we were trying to take a break, wanted to discuss the menu. Cat came in from a slumber party at a friend's the night before. Just as we were breaking apart to go about our days, I remembered to let everybody know my sister was flying in tomorrow. She'd ended up coming sooner than she originally planned.

"Tomorrow? That's awesome. I love Harley. She's funny," Cat commented.

"That she is," I replied with a slow nod. "I told her if she wanted to go into town much, she might need to get a car rental."

"She can borrow one of the resort trucks," Flynn replied. "We've got three. There's always an extra one kicking around."

"She can't drive a stick shift," I replied.

"Are you serious?" Grant countered, looking dismayed at this detail.

I chuckled. "Yeah. Not everybody learns these days."

"I've already learned," Cat chimed in. "I can teach her, and I don't even have my license yet."

"When is your driver's license test?" Daphne asked.

Cat pulled out her phone and scrolled through her calendar. "In two weeks. Please don't make me drive a stick shift for the test. I'm pretty good at it, but I don't want to screw up."

"You can take my car," Daphne offered. "It's an automatic SUV. Let's make sure you get some practice in that for the next two weeks." Daphne's eyes slid to

Flynn. "Give her a break on driving stick shift right now."

It's not like Flynn would say "no" to anything Daphne asked, so he quickly nodded. "Of course. You can be in charge of practice until she tests."

Cat waved as she left the kitchen and headed to the private apartment. "Be right back, just wanna drop off my bag."

The group gradually filtered apart until it was me, Flynn, Daphne, and Nora. Cat joined us again to eat, but she was busy voice texting with a friend, which was basically a phone call, but not really. Sometimes I felt ancient.

"You better get ready," Nora commented.

"Get ready for what?" I countered.

"Your sister. Last time Harley was here, she had like three potential brides lined up for you. They were all her friends. You don't think she's going to bring one, do you?"

I groaned, leaning my head back. After a deep breath, I looked toward Nora. "How would I freaking know? She might try to get on my case about it, but she wouldn't bring somebody with her without talking to me about it first. They'd need a place to stay. As it is, she's taking Elias's old room."

"About time he cleaned that room out," Daphne said with a soft laugh. "When's the last time he actually spent the night here?"

"I can't remember the last time," Flynn commented.

"Yeah, he's full-time with Cammi. I couldn't be happier for him," I offered.

Nora gave me a considering look. "What about you? I always figured you'd be the first to fall.

Honestly, I'm surprised you don't have kids already. You've got family guy written all over you."

Flynn nodded. "That's what I said."

I shrugged. "Maybe someday."

Nora grinned, a sly look entering her eyes. That's when I knew she had another point. "What about Gemma?"

A vision of Gemma flashed through my thoughts— flushed, her lips swollen from our kisses, and her eyes hazy with need. The other night it had taken all of my discipline not to take her completely. I wasn't about to share *that* with Nora. "What about Gemma?" I countered.

"Delia told me you took her to dinner the other night, and we all know you took her out for a flight," Daphne chimed in helpfully.

Of course, I should've known they would all find out. Not that I minded all that much. "I like Gemma," I said simply.

Flynn, who probably knew me better than anybody at the table, chuckled. "Diego takes things at his own speed."

At that moment, the resort phone rang, Daphne stood, hurrying across the kitchen to answer it. The group slowly filtered apart. I was left with Flynn at the table as I finished my coffee. "Thanks for letting Harley stay here," I commented.

"Of course," Flynn replied. "She's family, just like you."

"You might regret saying that, depending on how long she stays," I replied with a chuckle.

Flynn shook his head. "I won't. She's good people." He regarded me quietly for a beat before offering, "You know, your habit of playing things casual doesn't really suit your personality."

"What do you mean?" I returned.

"Just that. I know your ex burned you, with what happened with your parents' money, but you *are* a family guy. I'd hate you to miss out on that because you're a little cynical."

I shifted my shoulders and let out a sharp sigh. "Said by the guy who used to take cynical very seriously. Daphne's really softened you up."

Flynn shrugged easily, not even bothered by my observation. "Maybe that's what I needed. Maybe you should think about what you need."

Chapter Thirteen

GEMMA

I was leaving my last yoga class for the day, driving home and looking forward to spending some quality time grooming Charlie. I found that to be a soothing activity. The dashboard in my car lit up with an incoming call. My older brother's name flashed on the screen.

I tapped the button to answer the call. "Hey, Neal."

"Hey, sis. How's Alaska?"

"Beautiful. I hope you can come up for a visit sometime soon."

"I'm planning on it. I'd like to make it before the snow flies."

"How's life treating you?"

My brother was one of my favorite people. He was smart, kind, and funny. He was also a kick ass attorney and handled cases specifically relating to environmental issues, his big passion.

"Life's good. Busy with work."

"What else is new?" I teased in return.

Although I couldn't see him, I could feel his shrug

and hear his smile in his voice. "Fortunately, I like working. You got a minute to chat?"

"Of course. I wouldn't have answered if I didn't. I'm in my car, just finished teaching my last class for the day, and I'm headed home to take care of the horses."

"All right, then. I wanted to give you a heads up before you heard from anybody else." Neal's voice became somber.

An anxious foreboding slid like icy water down my spine, spinning around and tightening in my chest like a cold fist. "What's up?" I asked, my voice sounding tense to my ears.

"The DA just filed charges against Coach Winston. It's all over the news tonight in Portland."

That cold fist clenched more tightly in my chest and a familiar sick feeling coated my belly. "What?" My lips felt numb as I formed that single word.

"They filed federal charges against Coach Winston. It's a whole slew of them, some related to university code violations, and others criminal, including sexual assault against minors. It's a big case. I wanted to warn you before you heard about it on the news," Neal explained, his voice carefully level.

"Holy shit," I said slowly.

"I told you my contacts let me know they were working on an investigation. If you want to talk to somebody, you could give them a call. There might not be any charges related to your case, but you could be a corroborating witness."

My brother paused, and I sensed he was waiting to see how I would respond. I didn't know how to respond. I took a deep breath, trying to quell the anxiety spinning inside.

"You don't need to do anything," he added. "I

thought you might want to know that's an option. They put a call out for any other victims to contact them. If you want my support, I can reach out to attorneys that represent victims like you and put you in touch with one. I'd be happy to do that."

My brother's calm and measured tone let me know he was worried. It also reminded me yet again that I was the one in my family everyone worried about. I hated that.

I took another breath, finally replying, "I'll think about it. I never expected this to happen. I honestly can't believe it."

"What happened to you in high school, and the reports you and Janet filed *did* get the ball rolling. Even if it didn't feel like it at the time. He's been under scrutiny since then. Things like this take a long time. What can I do to support you?"

"You always support me, Neal. Just letting me know this was coming is huge. I'll think about what I want to do and talk to you before I do anything."

"Okay, call me when you're ready to talk on it some more. Should we talk about the weather now?" he teased, mentioning an old joke between us. Whenever things got tense, we tried to talk about the weather.

I needed that just now. "It's beautiful here today. I still haven't gotten used to the long days."

"What time does the sun go down there?"

"Close to my bedtime," I replied with a laugh.

My chest was still tight, and I felt a little sick, but I didn't want to process my feelings with my brother at the moment. He knew me well enough to know that.

"Send me a picture of the sunset one of these days."

"You got it." I turned onto the road where I lived.

"I'm almost home, so I need to go. I'll talk to you soon, okay?"

"Of course. Love you," my brother replied.

"Love you too."

The line clicked off, and the music from the radio filled the speakers again. I took stock of how I was feeling. I felt strange, a little scared, and a little relieved at the same time.

As I went through my evening rounds of feeding the horses, I was grateful for the activity. I needed something to ease the restlessness threatening. It had been years, and I'd done a lot of work to get to a place where I was calm and steady most of the time.

Yoga helped, spending time with the horses helped, and trying to find my own fresh start helped. Yet, there was one thing I could never do—erase the past. I wasn't trying to run from my past. I knew perfectly well that wasn't possible. But still, sometimes I wished some things had never happened.

I'd never expected my former high school softball coach to face charges. And yet, apparently, he was. I couldn't help wondering if he would slide out scot-free somehow. He had gotten away with his actions for years.

I had loved my team and loved softball so much. I didn't even realize I was being groomed. That was a word I learned after the fact. Coach Winston was charming and funny, and he coached my high school team to two state championships.

He was also the first man who kissed me. The twisted saving grace in that situation was I wasn't the only student he targeted. When I walked in on him with his pants down around his ankles and my friend with her face turned away, I'd been simultaneously struck with fierce anger, shame, and relief. The relief came from realizing it wasn't just me, that I hadn't been singularly responsible for what he did.

My friend and I agreed to tell our parents together. Our parents had collectively reported everything to the school and to the police, but nothing happened. *Nothing.* Happened.

Well, unless you counted the school hiring an additional assistant coach and establishing new rules that none of the coaches for any of the sports teams could be alone with any of the students at any point. Aside from just what a mindfuck it was to have a man who I trusted and admired violate me that way, the *nothing* that happened to him resulted in bitterness and an almost suffocating sense of powerlessness.

After that, my promising softball career that might have resulted in a collegiate scholarship crashed and burned. Although I thought it was crazy in hindsight, I had actually tried to stay on the team for my senior year. I got injured, and that was that.

That injury led me to yoga classes and eventually to what I was doing now. All along, the specter of what happened with Coach Winston was there. He never took things too far. It had only been three incidents. If there was such a thing as *only* in a situation like that.

I tried to act like a normal teenage girl. I tried to date. It wasn't horrible, but I felt so out of place. I never felt like I could relax with anyone. I went on to college and still dated here and there. Sex was a mechanical exercise of going through the motions.

And now, years later, Coach Winston was arrested. After his high school coaching career, he'd gone on to greater glory with a college team and another championship. I wondered if he would somehow escape justice again and slide out from accountability. With the increased scrutiny in the media of mostly men in power abusing that power in sexual ways, I remember thinking none of it surprised me. Despite the alleged greater awareness in our society around these issues, I had little faith genuine change would happen.

I gave Charlie a last stroke along the side of his neck before going to check on Shasta. With the other two horses owned by others, I took care of feeding them, but that was it. Charlie and Shasta were owned by the owners of the barn, and they'd asked me to spoil them accordingly. I loved it.

"Hey, Shasta," I said when I stopped in front of his stall.

He leaned his head over the stall door and nudged my shoulder with his nose. I stroked his forehead and slipped a treat out of my pocket. When I held it out on my flat palm, he nibbled it up. After he returned to chew on his evening hay, I made sure everything was put away for the night.

"Good night," I called as I left the barn.

When I closed the barn door behind me, I stopped for a moment, absorbing the sounds of night falling. The swooshing sound of wings beating in the trees nearby, followed by the call of a raven, and an owl hooting in reply. There were no crickets in Alaska, which I thought was kind of amusing. I hadn't expected to miss the sound, but I did.

My footsteps crunched on the gravel as I crossed the parking area over to the house. Scanning myself, I checked to see how I felt considering the news my brother had shared. I was surprised to discover I actually felt okay. The specter of what happened years before was something I had wrestled with already. Maybe, just maybe, I'd moved beyond it.

As I puttered in the kitchen, making tea and settling in on the couch to watch some television, I contemplated offering to be a corroborating witness if they thought it would help the case. I wasn't ready to make the decision yet, but I was standing at the edge of it.

I returned to the kitchen to get some honey for my tea. Opening a cabinet, I was suddenly struck with the realization that this very place on the counter was where Diego had sent me flying. He had done what I thought impossible. He'd made me forget myself.

Chapter Fourteen

DIEGO

"Oh, my God," my sister said, placing her hand over her heart for emphasis. "This is incredible, Daphne."

Harley, my youngest sister, took another bite of Daphne's concoction for the evening. She'd made this subtly spicy Thai stir fry with rice noodles, marinated chicken, and veggies. It was one of our staff evenings, and Harley's arrival was well-timed.

Daphne smiled at her. "Glad you like it. Diego is my best assistant after Cat. Do you like to cook as well?"

Harley shrugged. "I could take it or leave it. I'm pretty good at it, because our mom made us all learn, but I'm definitely nothing compared to you."

I chuckled. "None of us can compete with Daphne's cooking. We all consider ourselves lucky that she fell for Flynn and decided to stay here."

Harley smiled between them. "I'm so happy for you, Flynn. You seem a little less cranky." It didn't matter who it was, my sister was direct.

Nora almost choked on the sip of water she'd just taken. After she took another swallow, she smiled over at Harley. "I forgot how blunt you are. I love that about you."

My sister laughed, brushing her almost black hair off her shoulders after she set down her fork. Her eyes whisked around the kitchen. "This place looks great. The last time I was here you guys were still finishing up some of the work."

"There's always work, but this main building is completely done," Flynn replied.

"How long do we get the pleasure of your company?" Nora asked.

Harley let out a small sigh. "I don't know. Joe and I broke up, which is definitely for the best. I'm a little betwixt and between with life. Most of my work is handled online, so I don't need to stay in any one location. I figured I would come here and try to make sense of what I want to do next. Please tell me if I'm imposing." She did transcription and translation for medical companies and loved it because she said the tedium helped calm her down.

"Absolutely not," Nora said firmly." Just like Diego, you're family. Stay as long as you need. That bedroom doesn't belong to anybody anymore."

"What's the scoop with Elias?" Harley asked, glancing around the table.

"He fell in loooove," Cat chimed in as she walked into the kitchen, catching that question.

"Elias?" Harley's eyes went wide. My sister knew all these guys, and Elias, of course.

"True story," I said before reaching for my pint glass of beer and taking a swallow.

"Well, if Elias can fall in love, then so can you," Harley said, her eyes lasering on me.

I bit back a groan. "Don't start with that right away, please," I muttered.

Nora giggled, her eyes glinting with mirth as she split her gaze between Harley and me. "Diego went on a date."

I glared at Nora. "Is that necessary? If you keep this up, I'm not gonna consider you family anymore."

My sister smiled widely. "I'll grill him about that later. I have to be strategic."

"Fuck my life," I said, glancing to Tucker who sat beside me.

He snorted. "Dude, you shoulda seen this coming. Last time she was here, she was trying to sell you on a few of her friends."

Fortunately, conversation moved along. I always loved these nights where we could kick back in the kitchen and relax. Although being a bush pilot in Alaska was considered a risky job, it felt pretty low-key to me. After being on active duty in the Air Force, being able to hang with friends and know my biggest worry was related to the weather and how it might affect our flight schedules kept stress low on my radar.

Later that night, after those of us who stayed in the new staff house had decamped to the living room there, Harley filled me in on her messy breakup with Joe, her college boyfriend who she'd stayed with for no reason other than convenience as far as I could tell.

"I couldn't believe it. I literally walked in on him fucking Janine," she explained with more annoyance than hurt in her tone.

"Would you like me to kick his ass?" I countered.

Harley shook her head. "No thanks, bro. It's not worth the plane ticket to Texas. I threw my keys at him and scratched his ass with them. I didn't mean to, but it was still funny." She rolled her eyes and leaned back into the cushions on the couch. "Enough about me. Now, tell me about your date."

I knew she wouldn't leave that topic alone for long, so I was prepared. "Her name is Gemma. She runs a yoga studio here in town. We've only had dinner once."

That made it sound like not much, but I wasn't about to tell my sister about the kiss that blew my mind in the parking lot outside of the coffee shop. I also definitely wasn't going to tell her about the encounter when Gemma came all over my fingers in her kitchen. I confided in my sisters plenty, but I did have some limits.

"I want to meet her," Harley announced.

"Jesus, Harley. It's not like we're getting married. We had dinner. Once. Pump the brakes."

She sighed. "You need to settle down at some point. I feel like you're letting what happened with Deana ruin romance forever."

Leaning back into the couch, I ran a hand through my hair and cast her a glare. "No, I'm not. When the time is right and it feels right, I'll settle down. I've had dinner with Gemma once. Don't get so far ahead of yourself."

"You also took her for a plane ride. That's more than just dinner."

I couldn't help but laugh. "It is definitely more than dinner. Look, you're going to meet her. You'll be here at least a few weeks, right?"

Harley nodded. "Of course."

"Daphne and Nora are trying to work it out for Gemma to offer a weekly class here at the resort. So, if Daphne doesn't sweet talk you into doing a class in town, you'll meet Gemma when she comes out here."

Harley clapped her hands together. "Yes! I need to screen her. If she's secretly a bitch, then it'll be good to know right off the bat."

"God help me," I muttered. "Worry about your own love life, please."

"I've sworn off men forever. I only had to walk in on one boyfriend screwing my friend. That's enough to last me a lifetime."

"You'll feel differently after the sting fades."

Harley's brows rose toward her hairline. "You're one to talk. All Deana did was steal money. You haven't been serious with anyone since then."

———

Elias leaned against the plane wing, dragging his sleeve across his forehead. "Fuck, man. That's a lot of dog food."

I chuckled as we turned together to glance over toward the pallet stacked with bags of dog food. We were loading up one of our planes for a delivery run to the general store in a small village.

"It's always something. This isn't as fun as taking that rescue dog who got adopted the other week." Elias flashed a grin. "Thanks for helping me load up. You seem pretty close to one hundred percent," I commented, gesturing toward his ankle.

Early last winter, Flynn and Elias had been in a minor plane crash when a bird flew into one of their engines. Aside from cracked ribs, Flynn had been otherwise unscathed. Elias had sustained a nasty ankle break and gotten poked good and hard in the side by a branch. He'd been a cranky ass for a few months, but he was flying again and in love with Cammi, so all was right with his world.

Elias flashed a quick grin, his eyes crinkling at the corners. "Pretty much. I'm guessing I'll be able to predict the weather with this ankle for the rest of my life, but otherwise, it's all good."

I chuckled. "That's like my shoulder," I said, patting my left shoulder. I'd dislocated the shoulder during a training exercise in the Air Force—a total fluke. Ever since then, it felt okay most of the time and didn't give me any trouble, but I sure as hell could tell you when it was about to rain or snow. "What's on your schedule today?"

Elias glanced through the open garage doorway of the hangar out toward another plane already waiting near the runway. "I'm taking one of the tourist groups. Just a nice pretty flight over a few glaciers. Maybe the wildlife will cooperate for us."

We laughed together. That was a running joke. There was wildlife in abundance in Alaska, and for the most part when we took tourists on the "money trips," as Flynn called them, we usually saw some wildlife. Most often, we encountered moose, occasionally bears, and along the shorelines, the rare sighting of a sea lion from the air if they were in the shallow water, or resting on the rocks. We also saw rafts of otters, seals, puffins, and eagles all over the freaking place. If we were really lucky, we might see a whale breaching, or pods of orcas and beluga whales.

On occasion, we saw nothing more than common seagulls. "I'll be thinking positive for you. That one area, just past the harbor, has been a good spot for bears lately. I've seen one or two most every time we go through. I'm guessing a mama bear hibernated nearby over winter."

Elias dipped his head in acknowledgment. "Thanks for the tip. I'll make sure to keep to a low elevation in that area." Elias pushed away from the plane wing and strode to the pallet, hefting another bag of dog food on his shoulder to stack in the back of the plane. "Let's finish up so you can get rolling."

We moved quickly and had the pallet empty in short order. I waved Elias off when his group arrived. Only minutes later, I followed him up into the air, steadying the plane once I could level out. The small planes were so much fun to fly. You could see the world from above the entire time, unlike the big commercial planes where you got so high there wasn't much to see other than clouds.

Flying gave me a sense of freedom like nothing else did. I felt peaceful in the air, coasting along, savoring the view of the sparkling ocean below and the mountains in the distance. Mount Augustine, the volcano that stood sentry out in Cook Inlet had a halo of clouds encircling its peak. That volcano stood tall and majestic, a quiet reminder of its potential power at all times. It also served as the backdrop for some of the prettiest sunsets I'd seen in my entire life.

As I flew, Gemma came to mind. I meant to text her about dinner, but then Harley showed up earlier than I expected. I made a mental note to text her when I landed back in Diamond Creek today.

My mind shifted over to my little sister. Our family had always been close. We'd grown up blessed with two parents who loved each other. They'd fallen in love young, had kids and stayed in love all the way until they passed. I thought I was going to do the same thing until Deana notched a decisive scar on my trust.

I was more philosophical about it now than I'd been when it happened. I'd been too young anyway. Hell, I'd asked the girl to marry me when I'd enlisted in the Air Force. Deana had been Laura, my next youngest sister's, close friend. Of course, I'd trusted her. As soon as she got her degree in accounting, my parents hired her to handle the books for my dad's company. He'd done construction for years and ran a pretty good business. Deana embezzled a nice chunk, and they had to scrape by after that with my mom cleaning houses to make up the difference.

While I didn't like admitting Harley was right about me, she had a point. I'd kept my distance from anything serious after I broke it off with Deana. In a weird way, what Deana did felt more personal than if she'd screwed around on me. Maybe because it took planning on her part and happened over time. It wasn't a fluke, or a moment of reckless judgment. I was also intensely protective of my parents.

I kicked Deana to the curb in my thoughts. I didn't want to dwell on her. Gemma was much more appealing to think about. That girl had cleared out an entire room in my brain. She was already furnishing it and didn't appear to have any intentions of moving out soon. I'd replayed our encounter in her kitchen a few more times than I'd ever admit. The magnetic pull to her held strong regardless of whether she was nearby.

Chapter Fifteen

GEMMA

"And, here's the main room," Daphne said, gesturing with a hand around the large open space.

I spun in a slow circle. "This is beautiful," I said.

This was my first time visiting the resort. Although it felt as if we were truly deep in the wilderness, Walker Adventures was only twenty miles or so from Diamond Creek. The resort was a large octagonal shaped building with several stories. This main floor was an expansive open space with windows on all sides except one where it led into what I presumed was a dining area. The windows offered views of a field with flowers blooming under the late-afternoon sunshine, and evergreen trees mingling with cotton wood and birch. Beyond the field, the hill sloped downward, offering a view of the bay in the distance, and of course the mountains.

"It is, isn't it?" Daphne commented when I looked back toward her. "I feel so spoiled to live here and see this every day."

I smiled. "I get it. I feel lucky just to be here."

"We were thinking you could do the yoga class

upstairs. Follow me." Daphne gestured toward the stairs.

Although the main room had an open layout, it offered several areas for relaxing and mingling. There was a sectional in one corner that had a large flatscreen television mounted on the wall, and there was a reading area surrounded with comfortable chairs and low bookshelves defining the space. In another area, a smaller couch and chairs faced a large woodstove.

"There's a nice room upstairs. I think it's a good size for you," Daphne said, crossing over to a spiral staircase in the corner.

I followed her up, and we stepped into a hallway with hardwood flooring and rows of doors, basically like a hotel. Daphne glanced over at me. "These upper floors are almost all guest rooms, but we have a rec room on this level."

Following her to the end of the hallway, we stepped into a room with windows facing into the forest. The room was empty with the hardwood flooring echoing under our footsteps. "Do you think this is big enough?" she asked.

"There's room for about ten students. I can't imagine there would be more than that at a time. How many guests do you all have?"

"Up to thirty at any given time. But I think you're right. Only about ten would sign up. Plus, half or more of them are men."

I laughed. "Lots of men do yoga. You've sweet talked all the guys here into coming to my classes in town."

"We were actually thinking maybe you could do a class for guests and one for staff every time you were here. We'll still come to your classes in town, so you won't be losing the business. Obviously, we'd be paying you for the classes here."

"Sounds like a plan to me. On Wednesdays during the week I only have morning and lunch classes because the room isn't available in the evening. Why don't I just plan to come out then? If that works for you all."

"Perfect. When can you start?" Daphne asked, clasping her hands together in front of her chest.

"This coming week if you want. We could start with a staff class and then if enough guests sign up, I'll do that too. It's Sunday, so that would be in three days."

"Awesome. Now, do you want to have dinner with us?"

"As if I would turn down your food," I replied with a grin. "I've only had the scones you made for Cammi and a few things at her grand reopening, but everything was delicious."

Daphne's cheeks flushed slightly. "Thank you. Let's go back downstairs. I'll show you the kitchen."

A few minutes later, Daphne was showing me around the kitchen. Although it was an industrial kitchen and clearly designed to serve guests, the space was inviting. There was a large island with stools surrounding it with a view of the stove area, along with a long table by the windows offering a view over the field and mountains.

"Tonight's staff night," she explained while she checked on something Cat was doing on the stove.

Cat was Flynn's younger sister and looked so much like him it was endearing. Although she was a good foot shorter, she had his slate blue eyes and dark blond hair and a more feminine version of his strong features. "How does it look?" Cat asked as she peered into the pan with Daphne.

"Great," Daphne said encouragingly. "You want to keep it going until the glaze caramelizes. The heat has to be just right."

"What are you making?" I asked.

Cat looked up, her ponytail swinging with the motion. "Glazed pork with rice and spinach. It's a new recipe to me."

Daphne glanced her way. "You're a better cook than you give yourself credit for. Stop worrying so much. The only way you learn is to try new things."

"Plus, you have Daphne as your teacher. Rumor has it everything she makes is amazing," I offered.

"It totally is," Tucker called as he walked through the archway from the main room into the kitchen.

Like the other guys who flew for Walker Adventures, I'd gotten to know Tucker because Daphne brought him to my yoga classes on occasion. I smiled over at him. "Hey, Tucker, how's it going?"

His brows hitched up when he saw me. "Oh, the yoga teacher's here. Are you gonna make me do yoga before dinner?"

I laughed. "No."

I was relieved for the distraction of more people appearing. Diego had texted me to let me know his sister had arrived sooner than he expected. I was trying not to think about it and told myself it was no big deal to meet his sister because we weren't even a thing. Not at all. It didn't seem to matter what I tried to tell myself, anxiety pinged around my body every time I thought about it. I'd take any distraction I could get.

"Be nice," Daphne called over. "Gemma's joining us

for dinner. She is going to do one staff class a week out here though. You're expected to be there."

Tucker slipped his hips onto a stool by the island while Daphne started shredding cheese. "Yes, ma'am," he said with mock solemnity. "We do whatever Daphne says." He glanced toward me. "We want her to stay happy and keep making our food."

Daphne rolled her eyes. Nora entered the kitchen. "Hey, Gemma," she called over as she disappeared through a doorway at the back of the kitchen. It looked to be a pantry because I could see a glimpse of the shelves lining its walls. She reappeared with a bottle of wine and some glasses.

"Anybody want wine?" She stopped by the counter where Daphne was working.

"I'll take some," Daphne said. "I don't usually turn down wine."

"You?" Nora's eyes met mine.

I shook my head. "No, thanks. I'm driving."

Over the next half hour or so, the kitchen gradually filled with staff as they filtered in from wherever they'd been. I settled on a stool near the end of the counter, enjoying the banter between the group. I didn't have to see him to know when Diego arrived. The hairs on the back of my neck rose, and heat chased over my skin.

I couldn't stop myself from glancing over to the archway that led into the kitchen. His dark curls were rumpled, standing out against his burnished skin. My eyes lingered on him as he walked across the room. He was talking to Flynn who was handsome all on his own, but didn't have the effect on me and my hormones that Diego did. Good thing, seeing as he was absolutely taken by Daphne.

Diego's arms swung easily at his sides, and I

savored the flex of his broad shoulders with the subtle motion. He had on a faded black T-shirt, and I couldn't help but wonder what his chest looked like underneath it. Gah! I had it bad. When he looked away from Flynn, his gaze landed on mine immediately, as if he sensed I was here. For a split second, it felt as if there was an electrical wire connecting us, sparking in the air all the way across the room.

Dear God. My body needed a warning sign for this man. "Danger, risk of explosion." Or something along those lines.

Daphne said something to me, and I tore my eyes from his. "What?" I asked reflexively.

"I asked if you wanted one of these." She held up some kind of bread item she'd just pulled out of the oven.

"Of course. I don't even know what it is, but I'll take it."

Daphne grinned, a sly gleam in her eyes. "Rolls stuffed with brie and prosciutto." She paused, arching a brow. "Which you might've heard when I asked, if you hadn't been staring so hard at Diego."

My cheeks got hot when the man in question stopped beside me. "I'll take one," he said quickly. After Daphne handed us rolls on two small plates, he glanced to me when she moved on. "This is a nice surprise."

"Hi," I managed breathily.

"I should warn you, my sister is about to show up, and she wants to meet you."

Chapter Sixteen

DIEGO

Gemma's eyes widened as she stared back at me. She'd been about to take a bite of one of those rolls and lowered it slowly to the plate. "Soon?"

I nodded, trying not to laugh. I understood her anxiety because meeting my sister was akin to coming face to face with a freight train. There was no stopping her, and Gemma didn't even know that. "I did tell you she was already here."

Gemma nodded, popping one of those rolls into her mouth and closing her eyes as she chewed. I couldn't look away from the sight of her lush, plump lips closing around the roll. It didn't help matters one iota when she let out a soft moan of satisfaction, which sent a poorly timed jolt of lust through my body.

Opening her eyes, she swallowed. "Daphne's food is a religious experience," she said reverently.

I chuckled. "Agreed. You see why we're all so happy Flynn fell in love with her. We'll be on his case instantly if anything looks rocky between them."

I popped one of the small rolls into my mouth,

closing my eyes as the combination of flavors invaded my senses. "Fuck," I said when I opened my eyes. "They're just rolls, but they are incredible."

Gemma laughed softly, leaning her elbows on the counter. "They are. So, your sister. Where is she?"

I glanced at the clock above the stove. "She went into town with Nora earlier, but Nora's back, so I expect Harley to show up any minute."

"Do I need to worry?"

"Not at all. I have four sisters, and they all have opinions about my life. Lately, Harley has been on a kick trying to set me up and get me married off."

Gemma's cheeks went pink. "She wants to marry you off?"

I shrugged. "Yes."

"Is your family kind of old-fashioned?" she asked in between bites.

Tucker appeared at that moment, hearing the tail end of Gemma's question. "If by old-fashioned, you mean they expect everyone to settle down and be madly in love forever, yes, that would be Diego's family." He clapped me on the shoulder as he snagged one of my rolls and passed by with a wink.

I rolled my eyes as he retreated. "You owe me one," I called.

Tucker turned back, resting his elbow on the back of one of the barstools by the counter. "What do I owe you?"

"A roll. They're amazing."

Just then, Daphne bustled by, immediately hurrying over to the stove and pulling out another tray of the very rolls under discussion. Without a word, she stopped beside me and added two to my plate, casting a sly smile in Tucker's direction.

"Thank you, Daphne," I called. Daphne was always on the move and was hurrying off already.

"Seems like she does a great job of managing the kitchen and all of you along with it," Gemma commented.

"She runs a tight ship. She takes care of three meals a day. She seriously loves to cook. Cat helps out a lot, and I do when I have time."

"You do?" Gemma's eyes widened as she looked back at me.

"Of course, he does." My sister's voice came from behind my shoulder. She stopped beside us. "Diego is a really good cook," Harley said with a lift of her chin, as if somehow Gemma was doubtful of my cooking abilities.

"This is my sister, Harley," I said, gesturing to her. "Harley, this is Gemma. She's going to be teaching a yoga class here every week. Or, so I hear, right?" I looked back at Gemma.

Gemma set her now empty plate down on the counter and nodded. "For starters, it's nice to meet you."

"You too," Harley replied, although her smile wasn't the warmest. My freaking sister. On the one hand, she wanted to marry me off. On the other, she wanted to be in charge of whoever I dated. I couldn't win, so I mostly ignored her.

"As to classes, I'll start this coming week here. Just one evening. We'll see how it goes. Daphne wants me to host two. One for staff and one for guests. We'll have to see if enough guests sign up to make it worthwhile."

Harley's green eyes narrowed as she assessed Gemma. "If the classes are good, I would think so."

Gemma regarded her quietly. "I like to think my

classes are good. I wasn't sure if that many guests would be interested. I suppose it depends on why they're here on vacation."

Harley nodded. "I suppose so."

"How long are you visiting?" Gemma asked politely.

"I'll be here for at least three weeks. Then, I'll have to figure out what my next plan is. I dumped my boyfriend, and I need to regroup."

"Oh, I'm sorry to hear that," Gemma replied, her brow creasing with concern.

"No need to be sorry. I walked in on him screwing my roommate," Harley said dryly. "But that created two problems. I had to dump him and ditch my apartment. Fortunately, Diego offered the spare bedroom in the staff house here, so I have a place to stay while I figure out what I want to do next."

"What do you do for work?"

"I do transcription and translation for medical companies. Sounds kind of dry, but it's actually fun. I have a lot of flexibility and can make it work for my schedule."

"That's great," Gemma replied. "So, you'll be able to work while you're here?"

Harley nodded firmly. "Absolutely. I have two deadlines to meet."

Nora meandered over, stopping beside us. "Did Daphne give you the tour and discuss the schedule?" she asked Gemma.

"She did. We'll plan on one evening a week and see how it goes. I like the idea of offering two classes at the same time. That makes it more worthwhile for me to come out here."

Nora smiled. "It will work out. I just know it. I already checked with some of the guests here. They all said when they weren't scheduled for something else, they would definitely come to the class before dinner."

Gemma was drawn into conversation with Nora and some of the others, giving Harley the opportunity to offer her observations. Because my sister never missed an opportunity to share her opinion with me. "Gemma seems nice." I supposed I should be grateful she kept her voice low.

"She *is* nice, Harley. Don't grill her. We had dinner. Once." It wasn't as if my sister didn't know that detail already, but I saw fit to remind her.

Harley let out an aggrieved sigh. "I'm not going to grill her. I admit to being curious that you actually went on a date, but I'll leave it at that. Although, I think you should ask yourself why you might finally be interested enough in someone to break your stupid rules."

Gabriel entered the conversation when he spun on his stool where he was sitting nearby. "Rules?"

At that highly inconvenient moment, Gemma made her way back to us.

"Yeah," Harley said.

"I didn't know Diego had rules. I'm dying to know what they are," Gabriel teased, a wicked glint in his eyes.

"I don't know what rules you're talking about," I replied, keeping my tone casual.

Harley, because she never hesitated to provide her feedback on any situation related to me, offered, "Ever since Diego broke up with his ex-fiancée, he has a rule that he doesn't date. That's it. It's been that way for years now." Harley lifted her hands in a so-what motion.

"You have an actual rule?" Gabriel pressed.

I shook my head and popped another roll in my

mouth. I could use the flavor distraction with the side benefit that I didn't have to talk.

Harley twisted her lips. "It might as well be official."

"Oh, for fuck's sake, y'all. I don't have any rules," I finally interjected after I finished chewing.

"It is true that you generally don't date," Tucker chimed in as he appeared on the opposite side of the counter, swiping the last roll on the tray Daphne had left on top of the stove and tossing it in his mouth with a grin.

I looked amongst my friends, casting a quick glance at Gemma. Her eyes twinkled, and a smile teased at the corners of her mouth. I relaxed inside. Good, at least she could tell my friends and my sister were just giving me a little hell. Well, maybe not my sister. She had an agenda, always. "I don't have a rule, and enough with the group discussion," I said firmly.

Conveniently, time was on my side, and Cat called that dinner was ready. We moved as a group, all of us heading to the long table by the windows. I was pretty sure my sister made it happen, but Gemma ended up seated beside me. She smelled like strawberries, and I wondered why, but mostly I was simply glad she sat beside me.

Dinner was a relaxed and somewhat noisy affair. I loved it here. While we might be a hodgepodge group, we were a chosen family.

Later that evening, part of the group decided to go into town to see a band at Sally's, one of the favorite local bars. I didn't want to go to Sally's, but I *did* want to steal some more time with Gemma.

Chapter Seventeen

GEMMA

"Your friends are great," I commented, my voice quiet amidst the hum of conversation surrounding us.

Sally's was busy tonight, as it was every night. The local bar was in a renovated barn. One side of it housed a restaurant with the kitchen in the center of the structure and serving as a divider between the two main areas. The other side had a small stage for live music and round tables scattered throughout the space. The old hayloft above had more tables. The atmosphere was pared-down country.

I hadn't particularly wanted to come to Sally's, but Diego had invited me along with Nora and some others from the resort. Diego cast me a quick grin. "They are. They can be a bit much with their opinions sometimes."

"I imagine when you're that close, everyone butts in."

Diego lifted a shoulder in an easy shrug. "So true. I'm the first to stick my nose in when I've got an opinion."

"So, tell me, what was Harley talking about?" I

asked, unable to resist the question.

"You mean how she thinks I have a rule?"

I nodded. I *was* curious, more curious than I wanted to be. I liked to think of myself as a sensible girl, and Diego had me thinking far too many not-so-sensible thoughts.

Diego rolled his eyes. "To make a long story short, when I was too young to know better, I got engaged. Deana was one of my younger sister's friends. Not Harley's, but my sister Laura's friend. After college, she worked for my parents doing bookkeeping. She embezzled a bunch of their money, and I broke up with her. That's pretty much the whole story. In all honesty, I don't think we would've lasted anyway because we were too young."

"It's awful that she embezzled from them," I commented.

He shrugged, his lips twisting to the side. "It was, but they were okay. You have to understand my family. Growing up with them made me think I should settle down right away. We were tight. My parents got married straight out of high school. They were one of those lucky couples. They stayed in love forever."

"That's so sweet," I interjected.

"It is." Diego shifted his shoulders. "That's probably why I asked Deana to marry me. But I don't think everybody lucks out like that when they're that young. I was off in the military when I found out about the embezzlement. Harley's got it in her head that I refuse to give anybody a chance after that. I don't look at it that way."

I mulled that over and took a sip of my water. "When we had dinner, was that a date?"

I hadn't meant to address my curiosity so directly, but now the question was out there.

Diego's intense gaze swept over my face. "Yes, Gemma. That was a date. What did you think it was?"

We were in a crowded bar with music playing in the background and people all around. And yet, it suddenly felt as if we were all alone. Sparks shimmered in the air around us, and my breath became short. I swallowed. "I think I thought it was a date."

He leaned his elbows on the table, shifting closer to me. I could feel the potency of his presence, all raw masculine man. Gah! I wanted to climb on his lap and kiss him. I wanted his strong, sure hands all over me.

"Good. Because it was," he returned in his gravelly voice.

The sound of his voice slid over my senses, and my belly shimmied. He regarded me quietly for a moment before adding, "I didn't really want to come to this bar."

Disappointment stung me swiftly, a lancing heat followed by cold. "Oh," I said, leaning back in my chair. "You certainly didn't have to come on my account."

His hand curled over mine where it rested on the table, his touch warm and reassuring. "I came entirely on your account. I was looking for another excuse to spend more time with you."

A fizzy sense of joy rose inside and my belly spun in flips. I definitely couldn't catch a deep breath even though I could've used the oxygen. "Oh."

"Now, unless you want to stay here, why don't you let me make sure you get home okay?"

I was pretty sure Diego didn't mean he was going to follow me home and wave from the driveway. Need galloped through me, my heartbeat echoing like hoof-beats pounding on the ground. I swallowed. "Now?"

"Whenever you're ready."

Chapter Eighteen

GEMMA

My hands were practically shaking, not from nervousness, but rather from the vibration of anticipation spinning through my veins. Diego's comment, *whenever you're ready,* echoed in my thoughts. I hadn't been attuned to how intensely ready I was before this evening.

For the first time, ever, my mind wasn't getting in the way. When it came to dating and men and anything touchy, my mind was an absolute master at throwing up roadblocks, anything for me to trip and stumble. Nothing disastrous. And yet, always enough to take me away from sensation and to keep me thinking about out of place matters that had nothing to do with the moment.

Dwelling in the moment, particularly when the moment involved intimacy, had started to feel like something I would never experience. Aside from the obvious benefits to my body after my injury, yoga had offered me a space to learn to sink into physical sensation. That was a gift. Yet, I'd all but given up the idea that I could lose myself in sensation when desire was part of that equation.

Desire was an unfamiliar experience for me. I'd dated here and there in college, and I was no prude. Yet, it was a crushing letdown whenever I followed things through to the conclusion.

Now, with my piercingly clear recollection of my encounter with Diego on the kitchen counter, I thought perhaps I might finally see through to the other side of all of those letdowns.

Learning Diego had his own cynicism about relationships was actually a blessing for me. Because I wasn't ready to try to deal with tangled emotions. If this could just be pleasure and nothing more, without worrying about all the rest, that might be a heaven I hadn't imagined before.

The door clicked shut behind Diego at my house, and he stood there with one hand hooked in his pocket and the other pressed flat against the door behind him. He'd followed me home in his truck. He wore the same black leather jacket he'd worn when I saw him on his motorcycle. Apparently, I had a thing for leather jackets.

All I was doing was standing there, and I could feel a prickle chasing over my skin, the sensation of individual goosebumps ticklish all over. The air felt heavy, laden with an electric charge. We stared at each other, and it almost felt as if we were connected by an invisible wire, one that vibrated to the frequency of the heartbeat of desire between us.

The silence was broken by the distant sound of a horse neighing. Diego's brows hitched up. "Do they always greet you?"

I smiled. "Usually. I need to give them their evening hay."

"I'll help," he replied, pushing away from the door and opening it again.

I dropped my purse on the table in the entryway and walked past him as he held the door open for me. I felt his presence beside me every step of the way. Our footsteps crunched in the gravel. I was wearing a skirt with a blouse and cowboy boots. Normally, I would change before dealing with the horses, but it was late.

We stepped through the barn entrance, and all four horses poked their heads over the stall doors, looking in our direction. Charlie nickered softly as we passed him by. Diego greeted each of the horses with a murmured hello and a quick stroke, which only served to deepen my desire with the tiny wrinkle that my heart flipped over at his easy kindness to the horses.

He helped me toss the hay in their stalls. Afterward, I returned to the storage room to make sure the grain bins were completely closed. One morning recently, I came in to a mess left behind by a pair of squirrels. After a quick check, I discovered I'd left the lid on one of the grain bins loose.

Turning back, I looked over to Diego where he waited by the door. He had one arm above his head, his hand curled in a relaxed grip on the door frame. The position lifted his T-shirt slightly, and my eyes snagged on the strip of bronze skin between his shirt hem and his jeans. My mouth actually watered. Because I wanted to drag my tongue over that skin and taste him.

Although it was early summer, it was evening, and the nights were cool here in Alaska. The air felt suddenly warm as heat chased over my skin.

Speaking of air, I couldn't get much in my lungs when I tried to take a breath. So much for all those yoga classes. Maybe two feet separated us, and I didn't know how to close the distance even though I desperately wanted to be closer to him.

Because Diego seemed particularly suited to knowing exactly what I needed and when I needed it, his hand dropped from the door frame and tagged mine. He reeled me close in a smooth motion. In a blinding fast second, he spun us around. My shoulder blades bumped against the wall, and his mouth was inches from mine.

I could feel every thundering beat of my heart. As every cell in my body vibrated with the frequency of my need and the molten hot look in his eyes. I gulped in air with a rapid, shallow breath.

"Tell me, sugar, should I wait to kiss you?"

I shook my head immediately. Because I could not wait another second.

Diego made a low sound in his throat right before his lips dusted across mine. It was a glancing touch, a tease, and maybe a test. A little whimper escaped. His lips brushed across mine again, and electricity sizzled like fiery filaments through my body. Impatient, I arched into him, sliding a hand around to curl at the back of his neck. He took our kiss from a brush of contact into a full-blown plundering of my mouth.

Diego kissed commandingly, one palm coming up to cup my cheek as his thumb traced along the edge of my jaw. He angled my head to the side and deepened our kiss. His tongue swept in deep strokes, and I couldn't get enough of the taste and feel of him.

By the time we broke free to gulp in much needed air, my body was on fire. My nerves were alight, and my mind was hazy with a near frantic need. Need for more—more of Diego, more of the riot of sensation only he seemed able to set loose inside of me.

We stared at each other in the shadowy room with nothing but the soft glow of a shaft of light falling through the open doorway. His face was in the shadow, illuminating its strong lines.

I was impatient, my hips rocking restlessly into him. We fit together so well, his arousal was nestled just above the apex of my thighs. I could feel it like a hot brand. I could also feel the slick moisture of my own arousal, and hear my blood rushing through my ears with every beat of my heart.

Diego's eyes searched mine. "Gemma, I'm about to fuck you against the wall. I was thinking maybe the first time should be a little more comfortable."

I shook my head. Because the truth was, the prospect of being so overcome with lust that someone would want to fuck me against the wall was an insanely hot idea. Plus, I didn't want my usual anxiety to take over. I might get bored and start mentally reviewing my to-do list, feeling impatient and wishing it was over.

"We're not going anywhere," I murmured, right before I leaned up, tugged on the lapels of his leather jacket and brought him back to my mouth.

Another mind-melding kiss later, he lifted his head. "Fuck, Gemma, you make me lose my mind."

My body overflowed with sensation, and I shoved a palm under his shirt, letting out a gasp at the feel of his warm skin. His breath hissed through his teeth, and I saw the flash of a smile in the dim light.

"Sweetheart," he murmured when I rocked my hips restlessly against his arousal. "This—"

I shoved his shirt all the way up and dipped my head to string kisses over his chest. I heard a muttered curse and then I felt his hands slide under my blouse. I let out a moan at the feel of his palms on my skin, his calloused touch sending sparks scattering. Every touch from him was its own experience, each one opening a doorway into another room of new sensations.

It was a fumbled rush, but he got my blouse open and pushed my bra down, my breasts plumping over. He growled right before he dipped his head and caught one of my tight, achy nipples with his mouth. The suction had me crying out, as I pressed against the rough wooden wall behind me.

I dragged my eyes open. I needed more. I wanted him inside me. I could feel the hard press of his arousal, and I reached between us, deftly undoing his fly.

He curled his hand over mine, stilling it. "Slow down." His tone was ragged, but soothing.

He didn't understand how much I needed this. How much I needed the frantic quality of it. "I don't want to slow down," I whispered.

His eyes searched mine. We didn't speak, but he seemed to understand what I needed. His hand moved away from mine, and I slid my palm into his boxers, curling around the velvety hot length of him. I savored the way he groaned, biting out, "Gemma, you're killing me. You're so fucking hot."

In another fumbled rush, I shoved his jeans down just enough that his cock sprang free. Meanwhile, he hitched my skirt up around my hips. His palm smoothed over the inside of my thigh as he pushed a knee out to the side. That simple touch was such a seduction, sending sparks flying over my skin. My insides were liquid, and I was needy, so very needy.

Diego, being far more prepared than me, yanked his wallet out of his back pocket, producing a condom and smoothing it on, protecting us both in a matter of seconds. Then, he reached between my thighs, pushing my panties out of the way and let out a satisfied hum when he found my core hot, wet, and ready. I was *so* ready, more ready than I had ever been in my life.

"Oh, sugar, so good." He drew his fingers out and obliterated my brain cells when he lifted them and licked my arousal off, watching me the whole time. "You taste as good as I thought," he murmured, just before dipping his head and catching my lips in a lingering kiss.

He teased his cock at my entrance when his tongue glided against mine. I was on the edge of coming already, but it wasn't enough. I wanted him inside me. My hips bucked against him, and I made a restless sound in his mouth.

He lifted his head and tugged one of my knees up to curl around his hip. "Okay, sugar, this won't be graceful." A gravelly chuckle followed, and I thought I might melt on the spot.

"I don't care," I whispered. Because I didn't. I wanted it to be ungraceful and messy and hot, so hot that I burned in the fire of sensation.

He lifted me against him, using the wall behind us as a brace. I felt his thick crown pressing and then he reached between us to adjust the angle, right before he filled me completely.

I let out a tattered moan as my head thumped against the wall behind me. This, *this*, was everything. I was held in Diego's strong embrace with his thick length filling and stretching me. Pleasure spiraled inside me, the force of it gathering with every resounding beat of my heart.

Diego's speech was almost slurred. "God, you feel so good. Hang on, sugar."

He held still for a moment before he began rocking

into me with subtle shifts of his hips. Each stroke went a little deeper and stretched me a little more. We were pressed tightly together, and my clit was rubbing at the base of his cock with every nudge of him inside of me.

My orgasm struck suddenly, almost surprising me. Everything pulled tight like a knot of pressure in my core before all the ropes snapped free. I cried out and trembled roughly against him.

His lips pressed on my neck, open and hot on the underside of my jaw, as I felt him begin to shudder before his entire body went taut as tremors rippled through him. It was all over but for the pleasure spinning through me in echoes. He held me there against the wall in the dusty, almost dark storage room in the barn, the sound of our heaving breaths filling the space. I was awash in sensation, coasting on eddies of it as pure joy drifted through me. I had forgotten myself enough for this to actually happen.

Eventually, Diego withdrew and helped me put my clothes back into place. His gaze coasted over me. I probably looked like a giddy fool, and I didn't even care.

"How are you doing?" he asked, his lips kicking up at the corner with a slow smile.

"Awesome. I'm doing awesome."

"Well, that makes two of us then."

Chapter Nineteen

DIEGO

I should've gone home after that. That was usually my cue to leave—a satisfied woman, and me replete with pleasure. But I didn't want to leave. Gemma had this easy joy to her that I wanted to savor. Admittedly, I didn't quite understand it.

We went back inside, and she offered me some ice cream. There was absolutely no reason to turn that down. Then, she curled her hand around mine and tugged me into her bedroom, announcing, "We're gonna go to sleep."

This was the second chance I had to slip away. I didn't.

Sleep wasn't hard to come by after that. Hell, she'd blown my fucking mind in the barn. I didn't know how, but I'd known she didn't want to experience some kind of orchestrated seduction. She wanted that rough, messy coupling in the barn, so I gave it to her. I hadn't expected her, in her raw, primal pleasure, to reach in and set a hook deeply into my heart. I sensed it wouldn't be easy to dislodge.

I fell asleep beside her, listening to the even gusts

of her breath. Just when I thought my own brain was going to kick on and keep me awake all night, she hooked her leg over my knee and curled up warm and soft against me. I fell asleep.

When I woke up the next morning, I was disoriented until I looked around. I smelled bacon and maple syrup. The bed was ridiculously comfortable with a lightweight down quilt and tons of fluffy pillows. Gemma was nowhere in sight.

Rolling over, I reached for my phone on the table by the bed to discover it was only six in the morning. I had plenty of time to get back to the resort if I chose, or to shower here. I decided to play it by ear.

After I got dressed, I walked down the hall when I heard Gemma say, "Neal, I'm not sure I want to be involved in the case. I need time to decide."

There was a pause, and I kept on walking because I didn't know how else to play this off. When I stepped into the kitchen, she replied to whatever Neal said with, "I promise I'll think about it and let you know. I love you."

"Good morning," I called when she set the phone down on the counter.

She turned back, her brow puckered and tight lines around her eyes. "Oh, hey. That was my brother." She paused, closing her eyes and shaking her head slightly. When she opened her eyes again, her brow smoothed, and she smiled slightly. "I'm making breakfast. Pancakes and bacon. Would you like some?"

"I'll never say no to that." Because I couldn't resist, I crossed the living room into the kitchen where she stood by the stove and dipped my head to drop a kiss in the curve where her shoulder met her neck. Her hair was pulled up in a haphazard twist, and she wore an apron over her T-shirt and leggings. She looked adorable and absolutely delectable.

She flipped the bacon in the pan and angled her head up. Before I knew what I was doing, I was kissing her and she tasted delicious. By the time I lifted my head, I felt as if I'd tripped and fallen inside. My heart gave a tricky twist as I looked into her eyes. "Good morning," I repeated.

"Good morning. There's some coffee ready," she said, pointing to a coffee maker with an almost full pot and an empty mug sitting beside it.

I helped myself to coffee, and she told me where the creamer was. I watched her finish making pancakes, and we sat together at the table to eat breakfast. It occurred to me that this was the most domestic morning I'd ever had, at least since I'd been a kid in my parents' house.

"What does your brother do?" I asked conversationally while we ate.

"He's an attorney in Portland." She regarded me as she took a sip of coffee. Setting her mug down, she added, "I'm not really the black sheep, but maybe the gray sheep of my family."

"The gray sheep?" I prompted.

"I don't really fit in, but I'm not a bad kid. My parents are brilliant attorneys and my brother's also a brilliant attorney. I was supposed to be brilliant, but my dyslexia got in the way. It made for some difficult times in school before we figured out what the problem was. My family is great, so I only complain a little bit."

I nodded slowly as I absorbed that detail. "Families can be challenging, even when you love them. You met Harley, and she's not even the most outspoken of my sisters. I love all of my sisters, but sometimes they drive me nuts. I hope she didn't say anything out of turn when I wasn't paying attention last night."

Gemma laughed softly before taking another sip of her coffee. "Harley was great, and she didn't say anything out of turn. It's clear she wants to see you settled and happy, and I'm sure you'd like the same for her."

I considered that observation. "Maybe so, but my sisters tend to be bossier about what they think I should do with my life."

Gemma smiled, her eyes sympathetic. "Family is a good thing, even if they drive us crazy sometimes. It's hard enough not to feel alone in the world."

She stood from the table, glancing down toward my completely empty plate. I grinned and pushed it toward her and stood. "I'll help you clean up."

"You don't—" she began, quieting when I shook my head.

"You cooked me breakfast, and it was delicious. I'm going to help you clean up, so don't even try to stop me."

She cast me a wry smile. "Putting dishes in the dishwasher is tough work. Have at it," she teased.

I did put everything in the dishwasher and then followed her out to help her deal with the horses that morning. The second I stepped into that storage area room where the feed and hay were kept, my mind spun back to last night.

When I had her in my arms, against the wall, while I was buried inside of her silky, clenching channel. Fuck me. Merely thinking about Gemma coming all over my cock nearly made me spin her back against that wall all over again.

A few minutes later, I stood beside my truck and her lashes lifted when she looked up at me. "Last night was..." Her words trailed off, and her cheeks flushed pink.

"Incredible," I offered helpfully.

Her flush deepened, and she bit her lip as she nodded. "It was incredible."

"Was it incredible enough that we'll finally have that dinner?"

I watched doubts pass like clouds in her eyes before she took a quick breath and nodded. "Definitely. When would you like to go?"

"Any night I'm back early enough from flying, I'm all yours," I said, meaning it completely.

Gemma slipped her phone out of her pocket and tapped open the calendar, scrolling through it quickly. "How about this Friday? I'll see you at the class at the resort next week after that too."

"This Friday works. We don't do late flights on Friday, so I should be on the ground before five. I'll text you my schedule and meet you here."

Gemma nodded, and we stood there for a moment. I wasn't accustomed to the feeling I was experiencing. I wanted to kiss her. Hell, I wanted to kiss her and take her back inside and stay in bed all day. This was definitely not usually how I felt about a girl. But I already knew the truth—Gemma wasn't just any girl to me.

Stepping closer, I leaned down for a lingering kiss. When I lifted my head, my cock was rock hard and my heartbeat thumped out a driving fast pace in my chest.

"Until Friday," I said as I forced myself to step back, climb in my truck, and drive away.

Halfway back toward the resort, my mind got stuck on the conversation I overheard when I walked into the kitchen. What court case was she talking about?

None of this should've even mattered. It's just that Gemma was starting to matter, and secrets didn't sit well with me. I told myself that she didn't owe me any explanations and that it was probably nothing. But I didn't quite believe it because there'd been a thread of tension in her shoulders when I saw her talking to her brother.

I remembered Harley telling me that just because Deana pulled a fast one on our parents didn't mean everybody would do something like that. I tried to remind myself that was true. I didn't need to create a problem in my mind where there wasn't one.

Chapter Twenty

DIEGO

Gabriel attempted to slam the door of the passenger side of the small plane. It was a weak effort because the doors were lightweight and didn't give a satisfying slam. I put my headset on and ran through all the pre-flight checks quickly.

Only after we were in the air did I ask, "Why so cranky?"

Gabriel slid his eyes sideways to meet my gaze, irritation evident in the tense lines at the corners and the set of his mouth. He put his headset on. We had a private channel where we could chat when we were flying. "Nora and I had a fight."

That was the closest Gabriel had come to admitting out loud he and Nora had a thing going. They kept it pretty well hidden from Flynn, but not so much with the rest of us.

"About what?"

He was quiet for a minute and then finally offered, "I told her I never planned to get serious. I thought that was already obvious. She got really fucking pissed off with me about it."

"Ah, I see. You were planning for this to be a long-term friends with benefits situation?"

His sigh filtered through the headphones. "I guess I wasn't really planning. That's part of the problem."

"That, and you two are sneaking around like kids trying to hide from their parents," I offered with a chuckle.

He groaned. "I know. This whole thing came up because she told me she was tired of sneaking around and wanted to be open about our relationship. She also said she had feelings she hadn't planned on. I said we didn't have a relationship. That set her off."

"Nora's pretty awesome. Why wouldn't you want to consider something more with her?"

"Dude, you know my deal. After what happened with Greg, I'm all set with commitment and relationships."

I angled the plane, watching the sunlight glittering on the bay below us, spread out in its sparkling glory with the mountains hugging its edges. "Seems pretty cynical to me," I offered. "So, Greg screwed around with Elias's ex and yours. Elias has moved on. Why can't you?"

Gabriel chuckled. "Really? You're as cynical as me. Out of all of us, you're the most likely to fall in love and settle down like your parents. And yet, because your first serious girlfriend pulled a fast one on your family, you won't even give it a second thought."

Okay, that stung a little, but I absorbed the sharp blow. "Fair point. Maybe I'm trying to see past that."

"With Gemma?"

"Sure. Obviously, I don't know what's going to happen with her, but I like her."

"Well, that much is obvious," Gabriel replied with a sly laugh.

Our conversation was interrupted with a radio in about an extra pickup for some passengers who needed to get across the bay to Diamond Creek for a doctor's appointment. After that, our day was flat out busy, and we didn't dwell on our respective relationship issues. I did wonder just how tense things would be back at the resort when Nora and Gabriel were in the same room. But that wasn't really my problem. My only problem was curbing my impatience to go see Gemma.

My old habit of keeping my distance reared its head though. We landed earlier than expected, and I didn't know if Gemma was free. I didn't give in to my impatience and went out to the resort that night. I did make an appearance at dinner there, and Gabriel and Nora were icy-cold to each other. I wondered how long that would hold.

Chapter Twenty-One

GEMMA

I walked around the studio, putting away the yoga mats for students who'd borrowed them for class after wiping them down thoroughly with a disinfectant. The bathroom door opened, and Daphne stepped out, smiling over at me. "Thank you. That class was great tonight. I'm on my feet so much with cooking that my lower back gets really tight," she said, rubbing her palm over the area.

"I'm glad it helps."

"Would you like to grab some coffee and lunch with me?" she asked.

After a quick glance at the clock, I looked back at her and nodded. "Sure. I don't have another class for a few hours."

Daphne's green eyes twinkled with her smile. "Perfect. Let's go to Misty Mountain. I need to check in with Cammi about the new system we've set up for deliveries."

We walked out to the parking area together after I locked up the studio. "New system?" I asked as we crossed over to our vehicles. I tapped my key fob, and my car made that soft dinging sound.

Daphne stopped beside me. "Yes. We've coordinated to deliver pre-made items. We don't actually bake them, but the guys drop them off, and she bakes them. I just want to make sure the timing for delivery is working and that they're turning out well."

"Does that mean I get to taste one of them for lunch?"

She grinned. "Let's hope so."

With a quick wave, she hopped in her car, and I followed her over to Misty Mountain. I was starting to realize I could get used to the small-town life. It felt good to be starting to make friends and to feel like I could belong here.

My mother had called again this morning and got me thinking. My mother always got me thinking, bless her heart. She still struggled to understand how out of place I'd felt for so long. It was no one's fault. My parents and my brother were academic stars. I was bright enough, but it had taken too long to figure out my dyslexia and my discomfort in school for me to ever really bounce back from that.

Then came the nightmare of the one area where I had excelled in my life—sports—blowing up spectacularly. I still stayed in touch with a few friends from that time of my life, but our camaraderie and friendship had been stained by the actions of our coach. We'd never fully bounced back. Not to mention that not all of my friends shared the same thoughts about how it played out, which complicated feelings on all sides.

When people read the news about respected figures doing inappropriate things, many people assumed that otherwise kind and decent people will be concerned. I learned the hard way that's not how it worked. Some people refused to believe what happened no matter how much evidence there was. Some people blamed anyone who spoke up. The attention was intense and ugly. Even with the increased awareness in the media around these issues, things were still messy and complicated. There was always backlash.

I sighed to myself in my car as I followed Daphne into the parking lot for Cammi's new café. It was nice to be somewhere where everyone didn't know the headlines about my old coach and the whispered secrets about what happened. Even though that was years in the rearview mirror, the effects were a boomerang for me with the new case.

As I turned off my car, I gave myself a mental shake. I was going to live in the moment. In *this* moment, I was having lunch with a friend. A few minutes later, I was walking into the café with Daphne. Cammi waved from the counter ahead as she served a family at the front of the line. I glanced around, commenting, "This place is adorable."

"Isn't it?" Daphne agreed. "I love how Cammi's renovated it."

"I know she's the new owner, but what happened to the old owners?"

"I heard they moved," Daphne explained. Her gaze arced about the space. "I still can't believe they turned this old building into a café."

"These were left over from World War II, I think. There are more in the Pacific Northwest too," I said, referencing the Quonset hut, in which this café was housed. The cylindrical steel tube-shaped structure had been renovated entirely inside. Windows were cut into the sides with sheet rock on the walls. The space had a bright, airy feeling.

"I told Flynn we need to get some of this furniture from Jessa out at the resort," Daphne added, gesturing as we walked by a small round table painted with a sunflower.

"I think I met Jessa at the opening."

Daphne nodded as we got in line. "She has her work displayed at Midnight Sun Arts, that's a gallery by the harbor. She sells it online too. I think it was a smart move for Cammi to coordinate with the gallery for the artwork here. It makes it mutually beneficial."

"Like your baked goods," I offered with a grin.

She chuckled. "Absolutely. It's fun for me. I love to bake. Although it keeps me busy at the resort, my schedule isn't really that insane because we never serve more than thirty people at a time."

I stared at her, my mouth falling open. "I can't imagine cooking for thirty people, and I actually *like* to cook. You have my full respect."

She laughed. "I used to run a really busy restaurant in Atlanta, so thirty people seems very manageable."

"Oh, so you're a former city girl too?"

At that moment, we reached the front of the line. Cammi smiled between us as Daphne answered, "I sure am. Born and raised in Atlanta. What city did you fly away from?"

"Portland, Oregon."

"Is my coffee good enough to compete there?" Cammi teased, picking up the thread of our conversation.

"Absolutely," I said. "You have mastered the art of coffee."

"Speaking of coffee," Cammi began, "what can I get you ladies?"

We ordered our coffees, and I got a sandwich along with one of Daphne's dessert pastries. Before we stepped out of line to wait for our order at a table, Daphne commented to Cammi, "Maybe you can take a break to check in with me about how our schedule is working."

Cammi nodded quickly. "I can have Amy cover the counter, and I'll join you ladies. I'm actually starving myself."

Moments later, I closed my eyes and let out a satisfied moan. Opening them after I finished chewing, I said, "This sandwich is incredible."

Daphne cast me a quick smile. "It is, isn't it? This combination of a cranberry cream cheese spread with the pesto is better than I expected."

"Do you make these too?"

"God, no. I can only do so much. Cammi and I reviewed the menu options together, but the sandwiches are all her."

Cammi appeared with her own plate with the very same sandwich we had each ordered. She sat down, glancing between us. "How was it?"

"We were just marveling at how good it is," Daphne offered as I nodded in agreement.

Cammi looked relieved. "Thank goodness. I have to say when I took over this place, I was pretty stressed out about managing a kitchen. Fortunately, all of the staff stayed and they're great."

"That makes a big difference. You got off to a running start, and you're doing really well," Daphne offered encouragingly.

We enjoyed our sandwiches quietly for a few minutes before Daphne commented, "By the way, we miss Elias out at the resort."

Cammi's cheeks went pink. "Do you? I heard he lost his bedroom."

"Of course, he did," Daphne replied with a grin. "He's never there because he's with you all the time. Although we miss him, I'm really happy for both of you."

Daphne's eyes shifted to me. "Now, tell us how things are going with Diego."

"Ummm..." I began. Heat creeped up my cheeks as I glanced between them. "Why do I get the feeling that you two know more than me about me and Diego?"

Cammi, because she was nice and sweet, took pity on me and reached over to pat me lightly on the shoulder. "It's okay. You have to get used to living in a small town. Whether you want it or not, people usually know things. We definitely don't know more than you do though."

My cheeks were still hot when I managed something like a casual shrug. "Well, we were supposed to have dinner Friday, but his schedule changed, so I don't know when we'll see each other again."

Daphne's eyes twinkled. "I'm sure he'll reschedule that. Also, we don't know much. All I know is Diego likes you, and the guys think you're an exception."

"An exception?" I pressed.

Daphne took a bite of her sandwich, making me wait. I didn't think she was doing it on purpose, but still. Only something related to Diego could get me feeling this impatient. After she finished chewing and took a sip of water, she added, "Apparently, he hasn't been serious with anyone since some girl he was engaged to when he was younger. That was over a decade ago." She leaned forward, her eyes widening slightly.

Curiosity pressed at me, and I decided I didn't mind asking questions. If I was going to be the subject of gossip, I might as well gain as much information as I could. "What do the guys say? I know they're a tight group. They were all in the Air Force together, right?"

Daphne nodded in unison with Cammi. "Yep," Cammi chimed in. "They're like brothers. I don't know that much. Just that Diego is known for keeping things casual with relationships. Elias said it was huge that he even introduced you to his sister."

As if on cue, the door to the café opened, and Harley came striding in. She stopped, glancing alertly around the café, her eyes landing on us at our table in the corner. With a flick of her dark hair over her shoulder, she strode directly to us.

"Oh, God," I said, keeping my voice low. "Harley seems really nice, but she also seems to have opinions, if you know what I mean. What if she secretly hates me?"

Daphne gave me a warm smile. "No need to worry. We'll protect you. If you have anything to worry about, it's that Harley has an agenda to get Diego married. Flynn told me she's even tried to set him up with a few of her friends."

Harley arrived beside us. "Hi, girls," she said. "Rumor has it this place has the best coffee in town."

Cammi stood from the table, her now empty plate in hand. "Let's hope the rumors are true. What can I get for you?"

"You work here?" Harley returned.

"I own it," Cammi said, her cheeks flushing a little.

"Hot damn. That's freaking awesome," Harley said as she followed Cammi up to the register.

I caught Daphne's eyes. "Do you think she wants

to marry me off to Diego?" I was a little alarmed at the prospect, amazing orgasms notwithstanding.

Daphne chuckled. "I have no idea. Harley has a strong personality. Just hold your ground. And, trust that Diego likes you, no matter what his sister thinks."

A few minutes later, Harley returned to the table with a coffee. After a long swallow, she looked between Daphne and me, announcing, "This is incredible coffee."

"Agreed," I offered. "I've been to Seattle plenty of times, and it's famous for its coffee. Cammi's coffee could compete there, no problem."

Harley's sharp gaze, so similar to Diego's, shifted to me. "So, tell me what brought you to Alaska."

I breathed a silent sigh of relief. I could certainly handle this part of the conversation. "I won a trip here and decided that was a sign. I was looking for a change of pace, so here I am. I landed a job, which includes a lovely house where I take care of some horses. That helps me cover the bills, and I started my yoga studio."

Harley nodded approvingly. "Good plan. Now, how do you feel about my brother?"

Daphne nudged Harley with her elbow. "Lighten up. This is only the second time you've met Gemma."

Harley, unabashed, shrugged. "So what? Consider it a screening."

I couldn't help it, and I burst out laughing. "I'm being screened?" I asked when I stopped laughing.

Harley actually looked a little sheepish this time. After a swallow of coffee, she explained, "Sorry. I guess I might be a little too forward about it. Diego got screwed over once before. I just want to make sure you're on the up and up."

I held up a hand. "No need to worry, Harley. I know how to take care of myself, and I have no expec-

tations. Plus, Diego and I have only gone on one official date. When you saw me at the resort, I was there
to talk about doing yoga classes."

Harley shifted gears. "You're not gonna give up
that fast, are you? Trust me, my brother is *totally* a
catch."

Daphne rolled her eyes. "You can't have it both
ways, Harley. Either you're trying to chase her away, or
persuade her to fall in love with your brother. Pick a
lane and stay in it."

Harley laughed. "Okay, okay, maybe I'm being..."
Her words trailed off as she appeared to reconsider.

Daphne interjected helpfully, "A bit much?"

I snorted a laugh at that, pushing my empty plate
away. Harley cast Daphne a friendly glare. "Point
taken." She looked back toward me. "Diego is
awesome. That is all. If you break his heart, I'll kick
your fucking ass."

"I don't doubt it," I said with a nod. Oddly enough,
this interaction had warmed me to Harley. It was
obvious she cared deeply for her brother, and I
admired that. Family mattered to me, and it meant a
lot to know Diego had family who loved and protected
him.

Conversation moved on to lighter matters, with a
few people stopping by the table to say hello to
Daphne. She deftly introduced me to more locals who
might come to my yoga classes. Even better than that,
maybe I would make more friends. I was all about
that.

Chapter Twenty-Two

GEMMA

"Mom, I don't know that I need to feel more free," I offered as I adjusted the phone against my ear and stirred the pasta on the stove.

"Honey, I'm just saying it's a way to take back your part of the story. I hate how everything went back then. While I am absolutely furious that man was allowed to continue coaching and has since gone on to abuse other girls, I'm also relieved it's all coming out now. The truth will set you free."

"Oh God," I groaned. "Now we're back to clichés."

My mother was undeterred. "Clichés become clichés for a reason. Because they make sense, and they can be meaningful. I couldn't protect you from him before, and I wasn't able to make sure he was held accountable. I think it might be empowering for you to be a part of this case."

"Mom, I already told you I'm thinking about it. Give me a little time to decide. There's not a big rush. The attorneys on the case sent me a letter and let me know the schedule. The first hearing where I could even testify isn't going to be for three months. If that.

You're the one who always tells me how waiting for court takes longer than watching paint dry. It's highly possible it will get continued. I don't have to decide right away."

"I know, I know. I just wish—"

I cut in. "Mom, let this be something I figure out for myself. Please."

My mother was quiet, and I could practically visualize the disappointment crossing her face. She was the kind of person who charged at life, and I knew she wanted me to charge at this.

"Okay, I will. Just know we're there for you, one hundred percent."

"I know, Mom. Your support means so much. I need to go because I'm making lunch, and I need to drain the pasta. I'll call you in a couple days, okay?"

"Please do. Love you, dear."

"Love you too, Mom."

I had a respite from phone calls on uncomfortable and emotionally loaded topics while I ate my lunch before I headed in to my yoga studio for evening classes. I was looking forward to going out to the resort tomorrow for my first two yoga classes there. Daphne had texted me today to let me know the guest one was already full.

After I rinsed my dishes and set them in the rack to dry, my phone rang. Glancing down, I didn't recognize the number, but I recognized the Oregon area code, so I answered out of curiosity more than anything.

"Hello?"

"I'm looking for Gemma Marlon."

"This is her. How can I help you?"

"Excellent," the man said smoothly. "I'm Tom Johnson, and I'm an attorney working on the legal case involving Shawn Winston. You're listed as a potential witness, and I was hoping we could speak to you."

"I've already said that I'd like some time to think about it and I'll get back to you," I said, trying to keep my tone firm.

"To clarify, I don't work for the DA's office. We represent Mr. Winston. You were listed as someone whose testimony might be positive for our client. Your hesitation to be available for the prosecution speaks volumes."

My mouth fell open as shock slid through me. For a second, I was bewildered, thinking it was insane that they'd think any of his victims would testify for him. Anger and bitterness followed. I'd seen this kind of thing in the news, where they persuaded people to change their stories years later. I finally scrambled together enough sense to reply.

"I don't know what gave you the idea I would be willing to testify in any way that would be supportive for your client. Absolutely not."

The attorney didn't miss a beat. He replied smoothly, "Well, if you reconsider, please let us know. He is innocent of all charges, and we are hoping to present that case to the court and to the public. Please don't hesitate to call."

"I won't reconsider," I said firmly.

I hung up the phone and set it slowly on the counter before curling my arms around my waist and crossing the living room to look out the windows. I felt sick and cold, so cold.

"The nerve!" I muttered to myself. "How do they even know I haven't agreed to testify yet?"

As I stared through the windows, my eyes landed on the horses, as they almost always did. Shasta had his chin resting on Charlie's rump, something he did often. I took a breath and let it out slowly.

Without thinking, I walked outside, crossing the parking area into the pasture. I walked through the barn and into the paddock area adjacent to the pasture. I fetched some treats out of a small sealed bucket that was mounted on the outer wall of the barn, immediately beside the door.

The horses were smart. The minute they heard the sound of the bucket opening, their heads lifted and they jogged over.

"Hey," I said softly when they stopped outside the fence.

I gave all four horses treats and took a few minutes to scratch between their ears. I let Shasta nuzzle my shoulder and felt myself calm down. Time with horses was grounding, and I was grateful I happened to be home when I got that strange call.

After that, I climbed in my car and drove in to my studio, my mind spinning over what-ifs. The call from my former coach's attorney solidified a decision for me. I would testify as a corroborating witness. Whether or not it would be freeing as my mother hoped, I absolutely was not going to be part of letting my former coach get away with something. I would do everything I could to make sure he was finally held accountable in a genuine, meaningful way.

Chapter Twenty-Three

DIEGO

Harley tossed her cards on the table and let out something between a sigh and a growl. Glancing sideways, I asked, "What are you cranky about?"

"I never win," she huffed.

"You won last night," Grant interjected, apparently unaware of how much my sister did *not* appreciate being corrected.

Case in point: Harley's eyes shifted to him. "Thank you for clarifying that I won a single game. I don't know what I would've done without your reminder."

Grant's eyes widened, but he opted for silence. Tucker didn't even bother trying to hide his snicker.

"You're not supposed to notice things like that," I commented to Grant. "Much less point them out."

Grant shrugged easily. Not much got to Grant, not even my sister's pointed comments. He organized his hand while Flynn placed his next card down on the table.

"When do we have yoga class?" Harley asked a few minutes later.

Flynn answered, "I assume you're talking about

Gemma coming out here. She'll be here tomorrow night. Will you be at the class?"

"Definitely. Daphne says her classes are awesome, but that's not why I'm going."

Tucker rolled his eyes. "Do tell, then. Why are you going?"

"To spy on Diego and Gemma," Harley said, displaying not even an ounce of shame.

I shook my head, placing down my cards and bowing out of the round. "Spying? It's a yoga class. I don't know how much spying you can do."

"Well, you like her, so..." Her words trailed off with a shrug.

"So, what?" I pressed. "If you're wondering, it's not exactly helpful for my love life to have you monitoring everything I do."

"Ha! See, you said "love." You are taking her seriously," Harley said with air quotes before lifting her hands up in the air in triumph.

I groaned, glancing to Tucker who sat across from me. "Remind me to say no next time one of my sisters wants to come and stay for a few weeks."

Flynn chuckled as he won this round, quickly gathering the cards and stacking them together to shuffle. "Okay, we'll remind you. Then, you'll tell us family means everything. You'll also tell us you can deal with whatever they throw your way, no matter how much they pry into your life."

I laughed as I leaned back into the couch cushions. "True story. Family does mean everything."

"Precisely why all of us are waiting for you to take anyone seriously," Flynn returned with a sly gleam in his eyes.

"Busted. Gemma and I had dinner. Once. We're going to have dinner again though. I'd like to take things at my own pace if the group doesn't mind," I drawled.

I tolerated the continued ribbing that night, not just about Gemma, but about everything. Because family meant lots of teasing, and I was definitely not the only focus. I might bitch about it sometimes, but I loved my sisters, and I loved my friends. Family did mean everything.

Even though I played it off like it was no big deal, Gemma was like a soft breeze in my life. She filled all the spaces in my heart, even the spaces I'd thought were shut off and boarded up. Even though we'd only had one dinner officially, everything felt much deeper with her. It didn't help matters that I couldn't stop thinking about her. Not the way it felt to be inside her, or the way it felt to fall asleep with her wrapped in my arms. I was in danger of falling for this girl, and I wasn't quite sure she was ready, or better yet, if *I* was ready. I didn't like the tiny doubts that feathered along the edges of my mind over that stupid phone call I overheard.

I wasn't that guy, the kind of guy who believed he needed to know everything. I wasn't that guy who insisted a girl keep me up to speed on every detail of her life. But trust was an issue for me. The fact I was even wondering about anything with Gemma was a loud, blaring warning alarm in the back of my mind. She was starting to matter.

———

Gemma's yoga class for staff at the resort the following evening was an exercise in sheer distraction. Her tone was calm and soothing throughout the class, and she didn't lay a hand on me, not even once. And yet, every single time I looked in her direction, I remembered just how intimately I knew every curve of her body. I knew what she felt like when she flew apart. My body also knew what I wanted—more of her, and then even more. Getting Gemma out of my system seemed an almost insurmountable task.

To add to my distraction, Harley set up her yoga mat beside me. Throughout the class, she occasionally offered commentary. I loved my sister, but damn, she could be annoying when she wanted.

A little while after class, after Daphne directed Gemma into an available private room so she could shower and change, and after I obeyed my better angels and went back to the staff house to shower and change myself, we reconvened in the kitchen.

It felt as if she were my own personal true north, and every cell in my body rotated toward her. I could play it cool though. I sat at the counter, teasing with the guys and ignoring my sister's pointed looks. I couldn't tell if she wanted to grill Gemma and chase her away, or if she actually wanted me to have a shot. If she kept it up with her attitude, she was going to chase anyone away, even one of her friends.

I felt Gemma's presence like a soft spring breeze when she stopped beside the counter. Her scent spun around me. Turning toward her, my lips tugged into a smile instantly.

Her eyes twinkled when our gazes collided. Her hair was a little damp, and I wished I'd been able to shower with her.

"Hey," she said softly.

"Hey. The class was great."

Since there was no such thing as a private conversation around here, Gabriel chimed in, "It was. Are you actually gonna come out every week? Because that's fucking awesome."

Gemma smiled. "If the guest class stays filled, I'll keep coming every week."

Nora approached, resting her hands on the counter by the stove across from us. "That means enough of us need to show up too, right?"

Gemma cocked her head to the side. "I suppose so. But once I'm here, I'm here. An extra hour is no big deal even if it's a small group."

When I glanced to the side, I didn't miss Gabriel's hard stare at Nora. But then, it was hard to miss. She ignored him completely. The tension between those two was at its height lately. They generally tried not to be in the same room, which was probably for the best.

Nora's eyes bounced off of Gabriel, her lips twisting slightly and a flush cresting high on her cheeks. She whipped her gaze back to Gemma. "I'll be there. I'm also going to keep coming at least once a week to your classes in town. It's a nice change of pace."

Daphne bustled by with a platter, tossing over her shoulder, "Dinner! Since it's just staff, let's take advantage of the table."

As we crossed the room, Gemma asked, "Do you all usually not use the table?"

"Only when Daphne's not serving guests. When she's serving guests too, we usually grab what we can in the kitchen right at the counter."

"Not that anyone's complaining about that," Tucker chimed in after my explanation.

We sat down to enjoy a dinner of silver salmon with a lemon dill honey glaze and sautéed veggies and rice. In short, it was heaven.

"Oh, my God," Gemma moaned after a few bites.

"It's a good thing I'm not here all the time. I would definitely gain weight."

Daphne cast her a quick smile. Harley behaved herself during dinner, actually having a normal conversation with Gemma, and even getting some pointers from her on Harley's consideration of going back to college. She did well for herself with transcription and translation, but she kept toying with whether or not she needed a real degree.

"I don't know. I think a college degree is important in some fields. But for what you're doing, your work will speak for itself more than anything. I would only go if that's what you want. Because it's a lot of work. I have a college degree, and I don't even use it."

"Really?" Harley looked startled at that.

Gemma wrinkled her nose and shrugged. "Yup. I went into sports medicine and didn't really love it. I found that I enjoy teaching yoga more. I do apply the knowledge I gained from those classes, but I definitely don't need that degree to do what I do. I don't see myself going back to that work."

Dinner carried on, and I walked Gemma out to her car afterwards. Just as I was thinking I might follow her into town and sweet talk her into letting me stay the night, there was a loud snorting sound in the trees. Glancing sideways, I saw a mama moose with two yearlings right behind her dashing out of the trees. That was no big deal. It was the brown bear that followed that sent a prickle of icy fear down my spine.

Gemma and I happened to be halfway across the gravel parking area. We were between the resort and the vehicles parked on the far side of the lot. I grabbed her by the elbow. "Over here," I said quickly.

The only thing giving us a breather to move was that the bear was distracted. I got us between two vehicles. Gemma was tense with tremors running through her. "Oh, my God, oh, my God," she whispered rapidly. "After seeing one of those in the airport, dead and stuffed, I thought that was good enough. I was totally okay with never seeing a bear up close."

"Understood. Keep your voice low. We're gonna get in this truck."

The bear had stopped just along the edge of the parking area. Whether he heard us, or sensed our motion, his massive head swung in our direction.

Flynn came out on the porch at that moment with a twelve-gauge shotgun in hand. His eyes met mine, and he lifted his chin slightly.

"What should we do?" Gemma whispered.

I didn't answer. I simply curled my hand around the handle of one of the resort trucks and opened the door, practically shoving Gemma inside. I climbed in behind her as fast as I could, but it wasn't all that fast because the bear was charging toward us right when the door shut. Loose gravel pinged against the side of the truck.

"Oh, my God, oh, my God," Gemma repeated, her voice shaking.

"We're gonna be fine," I assured her.

Glancing over my shoulder, I saw the bear was now standing at the back corner of the truck. Flynn had the gun lifted and fired off several warning shots.

"The bear will leave, just give it a few minutes," I assured Gemma.

We had climbed into the truck quickly, and she was sitting with her hip half on the console. I gave her a little assist, and she settled into the passenger seat, her eyes wide as she looked over at me. "That was crazy."

"Sort of. Bears and moose are part of life here.

That said, that's the closest I've gotten to a bear. I prefer to see them from a distance."

I glanced back to see the bear still standing near the back of the truck. Flynn fired off another warning shot, finally rousing the bear whose heavy head moved slowly to stare at Flynn where he stood on the deck. We listened and watched as the bear slowly, taking his sweet time, lumbered away. Gemma let out a ragged sigh after the bear's rump disappeared into the trees.

She looked toward me again. "I don't think I ever want to get out of this truck."

I chuckled. "No rush. We're definitely sitting tight for a few minutes."

"Do you think those moose will be okay?" Her eyes were worried as she peered in the direction they had gone.

"Maybe. Maybe not. Those were yearlings, so they're not as easy for the bear to take, especially not with a full-grown mama moose to deal with. If anything, we interrupted him. He didn't go in the same direction as they did. I'm going to guess they've had enough time to put some distance between them and him."

"Do you know if it's a male?" Her gaze swung back to me.

"I have no clue, really, but this would be the time of year that the females have cubs. Since there aren't any in sight, I'm going to guess it's a male."

My phone vibrated in my jeans pocket. I slipped it out as I leaned back in the seat. Glancing at the screen, I saw it was Flynn, likely calling me from the porch. Sliding my thumb across the screen, I answered, "Good work."

Flynn chuckled. "I'm glad the warning shots

chased him off. I'm assuming you're not getting out of the truck anytime soon."

"We're going to sit tight for a little bit."

"Is Gemma okay?"

Glancing to her, I said, "Flynn wants to know how you're doing."

"I'm fine. Now." She shook her head, still looking a little startled at the fast chain of events.

"She's fine, if you didn't hear her answer. If anyone else inside was planning on leaving, they should probably wait a few."

"Of course. Talk when you come back in."

I set the phone on the dashboard, glancing into the trees where the bear had disappeared.

"How long should we wait?" Gemma asked.

I shrugged. "Maybe five minutes or so. Enough time that we know he's not coming back."

She leaned her head back against the seat, rolling it sideways to look at me. "That was enough excitement for me this evening."

All we were doing was sitting in a truck. It wasn't even my truck. Our reasons for being here were amusing and slightly life-threatening, although the threat had definitely passed. None of that mattered. A switch had been flipped in my body.

We stared at each other, and it felt as if desire slipped through every crevice around the edges of the windows and doors like smoke, filling the air around us with a hum of electricity and sparks. Gemma's eyes darkened, a reflection of the raw desire coursing through me. I needed to kiss her as much as I needed air.

So, I did. I leaned over the console, sliding my hand around to cup her jaw and tracing my thumb over her bottom lip. We stared at each other in the quiet. The anticipation wound tight. It felt as good as I knew it would be when my lips finally touched hers. The sound of her breath catching in her throat was like a whip cracking through the air. Our lips molded together, and electricity sizzled through me in a fiery jolt.

Gemma sighed, her mouth opening the moment my tongue slid across the seam of her lips. Her tongue glided against mine in a silken tease. I dove into the warm sweetness of her mouth, savoring every little sound she made and letting out a rough growl.

Chapter Twenty-Four

GEMMA

Kissing Diego was heaven. I forgot everything but the feel of his tongue twining with mine, and his lips commanding mine with little nips and kisses at the corners before he dove back in. I never knew kisses could be pure intoxication. It felt as if Diego himself were a drug, and I had a straight line to his very essence. Kisses with him weren't a means to an end. I dwelled entirely in this moment, lost in the delicious seduction of his mouth.

I even forgot where we were. Until there was a loud knocking sound at the back of the truck. I didn't even know whose truck we were in.

We broke apart, both of us gulping in deep lungfuls of air. "Break it up, you two," a man's voice called.

Diego chuckled, casting me a sheepish look. "Sounds like Grant needs this truck."

"Is this his truck?" I asked, scrambling to gather my brain cells back into some sort of functioning mass.

"It's a resort truck, but he drives it the most, and he's definitely the one banging on the back."

"Oh, my God," I groaned, leaning my face forward into my hands.

"It's just a kiss," Diego said, and I felt his hand slide down my back in a comforting caress.

I lifted my head. "I don't usually get so caught up in making out with someone that I forget where I am."

"You and me both, sugar. It's been long enough that we should be in the clear as far as the bear's concerned, so why don't I finish walking you to your car?"

I gathered my dignity and climbed out of the truck. Grant was, in fact, standing at the back of the truck. Along with Flynn, Daphne, Tucker, Nora, and even Harley. Great, just fucking great. Now Diego's sister knew I was making out with him like a foolish girl.

Tonight?

That was Diego's text. One word. Apparently, that was all it took to set my heart to fluttering in my belly and heat spinning through my veins and creating a fizz of excitement in my system.

There was absolutely no chance I was going to say no. Because I was a foolish girl when it came to Diego. This was a strange experience for me. Because of what happened in high school, I'd skipped over having youthful crushes and all that fun stuff. Maybe I was getting the chance now. Even though I didn't know how this was going to play out, my expectations were so low that I was just going to grab onto this chance with Diego with both hands.

I tapped out my reply. *Where and when?*

Diego: *The brewery? Say, 6?*

Me: *Sounds good.*

My arms were wrapped around Diego's waist, and cool ocean air tugged at the ends of my hair. He angled the motorcycle into a corner along the road that flanked a bluff, offering an absolutely spectacular view of Kachemak Bay. Nature outdid herself here in Alaska, being all showy almost everywhere you looked.

We were on the way home from that long promised second dinner date, and I was beyond pleased that Diego had picked me up on his motorcycle. It was a small thing, but it was a thrill for me. Diego was plenty sexy without the prop of a motorcycle. Yet, Diego with a black leather jacket over a black T-shirt with black jeans and battered boots to match had my girly parts going into overdrive like cheerleaders at a winning game.

My cheek was pressed against his back, and I savored the feel of the air ruffling the ends of my hair just below the edge of the helmet. We weren't going that fast. There was really nowhere around Diamond Creek where someone could go fast on a motorcycle. Not anyone with sense. The roads were too narrow and winding. I loved the feeling of freedom on a motorcycle. The experience was very different, and yet it held similarities to riding a horse.

The local brewery restaurant had been delicious. I was discovering that, although Diamond Creek was a small town, the tourists that crowded the town in the summer brought things up a notch. There was plenty of excellent food from casual fare and even close to fancy. With the exception that I didn't think a single restaurant in the entire state of Alaska required fancy dress for dinner. Alaskan residents would probably boycott if that were the case.

Diego slowed as we approached the road that led
to my place, and I giggled to myself as we drove past
the very spot he had stopped to help me when Charlie
got loose. A moment later, he turned down my
driveway.

I reluctantly climbed off the motorcycle. Being
plastered to Diego felt good. Not simply good, it felt
freaking awesome. I took off my helmet and handed it
to him as he opened the small compartment behind
the seat where I'd been riding and stowed it.

Charlie nickered softly from where he stood by the
edge of the pasture fence adjacent to the parking area.
Shasta joined him, looking expectantly toward us with
his ears perked forward as Diego and I stood beside
his motorcycle. I shifted on my feet to look over, my
heel catching on a small rock. When I stumbled, just
barely, Diego placed his hand on my shoulder to
steady me.

It was nothing more than an incidental touch. And
yet, all of my attention swiveled to that spot, like he'd
burned a brand on me. Heat radiated from his touch
through my clothing, to my skin before sending a flash
throughout my entire system.

"Are they hungry?" he asked with a smile, the heat
banked in his eyes sending the butterflies in my belly
into a tizzy.

His palm slid away from my shoulder, and I missed
his touch instantly. I forced myself to focus and
behave normally. He didn't appear addled out of his
mind with lust. As if to drag my mind back to reality,
Charlie nickered again, this time with a touch of
impatience.

"Probably. My yoga class finished only half an hour
before you picked me up for dinner, so I'm a little late
with feeding them."

"I'll help," he offered, nudging his chin in the direction of the horses.

"You don't mind?"

"Of course, I don't mind. I like horses. Come on. No sense in making them wait any longer."

Diego caught my hand in his as we crossed the parking area into the barn. I gestured for him to follow me into the feed room. "We're not just putting them to bed. I need to get their food in their stalls first."

As I turned, I caught him glancing toward the very spot on the wall by the door where I'd gone a little crazy and he had fucked me up against the wall. When his eyes met mine, my cheeks got hot.

"Just tell me what to do," he said, his lips twitching with a smile.

It felt as if his words held a double entendre. However, because I was anything but cool, I simply told him what to do about getting the food ready for the horses.

"Shasta gets some medicine in his feed," I said, gesturing toward the buckets lined up in a row by the door.

It had taken me a few weeks, but I settled on a system where after I fed the horses in the morning, I brought their feed buckets in here because it minimized me carting things back and forth. "The food for Hazelnut is high end," I explained, referring to one of the boarding horses and pointing to a labeled bucket.

"It's vegan," I added when Diego peered into it, his brows hitching up in question.

"Vegan, it is," he said with a shrug.

After we got the feed buckets in the stalls, I let the horses in while Diego tossed hay into each stall. "What now?" he asked.

"I usually leave them to eat for at least an hour. They might finish sooner, but then I let them out for a few more hours before bringing them in for the night."

"An hour is plenty of time."

Reaching out, he caught my hand in his, reeling me close. In a hot second, sparks were scattering through my body. I was pressed against his hard, muscled form, and he dropped hot kisses along my neck while I shivered all over.

I was terrible at playing it cool, absolutely pathetic. And, apparently, when a man could *really* get to me, like only Diego could, I melted into a needy girl at nothing more than a few kisses.

"Plenty of time for what?" I asked breathlessly.

Diego lifted his head. "I'm reconsidering if it's enough time."

"You didn't answer my question," I said as he turned.

Disappointment sliced through me when he stepped away and reached for my hand. I wanted more kisses and more of, well, just *more*. He began to stride quickly out of the barn, making sure to pause and close the door completely behind us.

"For me to ravish you."

"Ravish?"

He flashed a grin at me, sending my belly into spins. "I've never actually used the word ravish."

I giggled, stumbling a little as we almost ran across the parking lot. We climbed the steps, and when I stumbled again, Diego steadied me with his palms curled on my waist.

"Wait."

It was one word from him, a simple request, but it felt like a command. I obeyed instantly, stopping and glancing over my shoulder at him. He was one step below me, and I began to turn.

"Stay right there," he ordered.

His hands slid down, coming to rest on my hips just below the curve of my waist. I held still, almost vibrating with need. I could feel the slick arousal between my thighs and was almost startled to notice it. I didn't even usually get too turned on, much less when I was climbing up the stairs.

One of his hands shifted, stealing under the hem of my blouse and pushing my camisole up slightly. I felt a hot kiss land at the base of my spine, that one touch feeling like a drop of warm honey on my skin. Another one followed and then another, as he pushed the fabric up. My knees felt rubbery, and I could hardly catch my breath as my pulse spun off wildly, like horses let out to pasture with their hooves pounding on the ground.

I distantly heard myself whimper when another hot kiss landed on my skin. He drew back, and I missed his touch acutely. "Diego." His name was a whispered plea.

Then, we were moving swiftly, stumbling through the front door. The next few moments were a jumble of my senses absorbing one thing after another. The front door slamming. Our clothes falling in a mixture of sounds—the thump of a shoe, my blouse whooshing through the air, and its almost silent rumple on the floor. Diego's palms on my skin, his lips impatient and teasing on my neck.

I was barely conscious, made of nothing but sensation and the intense craving for more, more, more— more of everything, and all of it related to Diego and his magic touch.

Somehow, we stumbled into my bedroom. The motion sensor lights flicked on, casting the room in a soft, ambient radiance. Diego spun me around right as we reached the foot of my bed. My breath was coming in ragged, shallow heaves. I stared at him, feeling a little wild inside, like a stream rushing over a cliff after the first thaw of spring.

"You're so fucking beautiful,' he growled, dipping his head and giving me a rough kiss. One of his hands splayed across my belly possessively and the other cupped a breast, his thumb teasing over my achy nipple. I was a little surprised to discover I was already completely naked.

I wasn't so out of it that I hadn't known we were getting undressed, it's just I'd lost track of the details. Diego was naked too, and I felt the velvety brush of his arousal, hot against the edge of my hip. The core of me clenched, and I wanted him inside me. *Now.*

Impatient, I reached between us, curling my palm over his silken shaft. His cock pulsed under my touch, and a thrill raced down my spine at realizing my touch affected him that way.

"Slow down, I don't want to rush this time," he murmured against my skin, his words and the motion of his lips another sensation that ricocheted through me.

My need was a bonfire with each sensation another match thrown into the raging inferno inside. I made a sound of protest, but he chuckled. "I'm in charge this time."

Impatient though I was, I would surrender to Diego because I trusted him that completely, and I wanted him that fiercely.

He spread me out on the bed, his lips blazing a meandering trail over my breasts and my belly. Sparks scattered over the surface of my skin as he pushed my thighs apart with a slow, almost lazy pressure. Then, he trailed lingering kisses on the inside of my thighs, and I trembled with an anticipation so intense that by the time he licked into my folds, I cried out sharply.

I felt one finger and then another sink into me, and my hips rocked restlessly into him as he made love to me with his mouth and fingers and drove me completely out of my mind. I didn't know how long I lasted before the pressure gathering inside me crashed like a wave, pleasure rolling through me in intense spasms.

I was still reverberating from that first climax when I felt him shift and rise up. My eyes flew open. "Where are you going?" I asked hoarsely.

"I have to find my jeans. Need a condom."

He was gone in a flash. Back before I could protest any further, he was smoothing a condom on, protecting us in a moment of liquid intensity.

I welcomed his weight coming down over me, savoring the press of his thick crown at my entrance and then the slow slide when he filled me.

His hand brushed my tangled hair away from my forehead as he murmured, "I want to see you."

Chapter Twenty-Five
DIEGO

Gemma's eyes opened slowly, her lashes swinging up. She stared at me, her gaze dark. I could feel the pounding of her heartbeat against mine. Her body still trembled from the aftershocks of her climax moments earlier, clenching slightly around my cock.

Her tongue darted out, and she dragged it slowly across her bottom lip before she took in a ragged breath. Then, I was kissing her, taking slow sips from her sweet mouth as I began to sink into her snug, satiny core.

Being inside her had me cast adrift in a river of pleasure. I felt fire licking at the edges of me with every stroke into her. Her legs tightened around my hips, and her skin was damp as I pumped into her. I needed air, so I lifted my head. Her eyes opened, and I felt the tension gathering in her again, every muscle tightening and rippling. It was all over but for the shuddering then.

Reaching between us, I teased my fingers over her clit, savoring the ragged cry of my name as she trembled through an abrupt orgasm. My own was hovering, like a snake waiting to strike. The pressure tightened at the base of my spine, followed by a fiery sizzle upward, and then finally my release slammed through me as I shuddered inside her.

I fell against her roughly, barely aware enough to roll us to the side and hold her tight in my arms as I tried to catch my breath. As my awareness filtered in fragments, I savored the feel of her soft curves against me and the gust of her breath against my shoulder. I let my fingers trail through her hair and shifted so I was propped against the pillows with her still in my arms. I felt greedy and didn't want to let her go.

Eventually, she lifted her head. "Do you think that was an hour?"

It took me a minute to catch up to what she was referencing, and then I chuckled. "I doubt it. When it comes to you, finesse is not my thing, nor is taking my time, apparently."

She bit her lip, her cheeks going a little pink. "You sort of took your time."

I leaned forward, kissing her again. My cock, still inside her, twitched slightly.

Much too soon, she reminded me she needed to let the horses back out. We took a quick shower, tugged on our clothes and went out to let them back into the pasture.

After we returned to the house, I learned she loved sci-fi movies. We watched one before we put the horses away for the night. I considered ravishing her in the feed room again, but I decided the bed was actually more comfortable.

I had another best sleep of my life after that. I could get seriously used to spending more nights with Gemma.

The next morning, she was on the phone again as I

came down the hallway to the kitchen. Yet again, my curiosity perked its ears.

"Neal, I appreciate your help, but I've got this. I'm going to call the DA's office and let them know I'll be willing to testify. If I need more support, I'll let you know."

Why the hell was she talking about attorneys and testimony? I hated the doubts that pricked my thoughts. I didn't want to be nosy, so I didn't ask. I sat down and had another nice breakfast. I couldn't resist giving her a lingering kiss when she stood beside my motorcycle before I left.

I returned to the resort, wondering about texting Gemma and asking if I could see her that night. With my current living situation, it wasn't that I couldn't bring someone out here, but it was a guaranteed way to make anyone feel like they were under the microscope. I had three nosy guy friends, and an even nosier sister living with me.

I had barely gotten into the kitchen at the resort to grab another cup of coffee when Harley came barreling out of the pantry. "Why the hell is an attorney calling me?"

"How should I know? And why the hell are you asking me?" I finished filling my coffee and set the pot back on the warmer. Turning, I rested my hips against the counter and took a swallow.

"Some attorney left me a message about a matter pertaining to Gemma."

I lowered my coffee, and icy dread slid down my spine. "What?"

Harley handed me her phone, tapping the screen to open her voicemail and hit play.

"I'm looking for Harley Jackson. This is Tom Johnson, an attorney based in Portland. I understand you're familiar with Gemma Marlon. We have a question about a legal case pertaining to her and are hoping you might be able to provide some information."

"What the fuck?" I muttered as she hit the stop button and closed her phone.

"That's my train of thought," Harley said dryly.

I pulled my phone out and was about to call Gemma when Harley placed her hand on my forearm. "Don't call her yet. We need to find out what the situation is."

Daphne came walking in the kitchen, her alert gaze whisking around the room. "What's up?" she asked, making a beeline for the coffee and pouring herself a cup.

"I got a really weird message about Gemma," Harley explained. She replayed the message for Daphne.

Daphne's brow furrowed as she divided her concerned gaze between us. "This seems really weird. You've only known Gemma since you've been here, right?" She directed her question to Harley.

"Yeah, why would they call me? All I know is Diego has the hots for her, and she teaches a really good yoga class."

I hated the way I felt, confused and filled up with questions.

"I think we need to talk to Gemma," Daphne said firmly.

"I don't think so," Harley interjected, shaking her head quickly. "What do you know about her?"

Daphne wasn't easily cowed and gave my sister a sharp look. "Not a lot, but I trust her. This strikes me as odd. There's no sensible reason for someone to call you unless it's not on the up and up."

Harley wrinkled her nose and blinked. "Okaa-ay. Should we tell Gemma about the message?"

"Are you going to call her?" Daphne asked, looking to me.

The lingering feelings of amazing-ness that had been clinging to me after my night with Gemma had dissipated. I felt as if someone had dumped ice water on me. Obviously, Gemma had no way of knowing this about me. I had a giant button about trust when it came to women, and it had just been pressed. Hard.

"I don't know if I should," I finally replied, feeling kind of like an asshole.

Daphne stared at me, a hint of confusion swirling in her eyes. "I thought you were seeing her."

"We've had two dinner dates," I said, now feeling like even more of an ass. While that was technically true, what had passed between us was far more than casual. That was my whole problem now.

Daphne's brows hitched up, and even Harley looked askance at me. Daphne shrugged. "Well, I consider Gemma a friend, so I'll be calling her. Since apparently this is none of your business, you don't need to be a part of that call."

Daphne walked off with a dismissive flick of her fingers over her shoulder. Every now and then, she reminded me precisely why Flynn had given her the nickname princess. I wanted to run after her and tell her I'd call Gemma about it, but now I felt like a heel. Annoyed with myself and the situation, I lifted my coffee mug and drained it quickly before leaving the room. I didn't have much time this morning before I needed to get out to the airport. I'd needed a change of clothes and my gear bag, so I'd come home. I was regretting it now.

Chapter Twenty-Six

GEMMA

"I'm sorry, can you say that again?" I asked, adjusting my phone in my hand.

"Harley got a really weird message," Daphne explained. "Here's exactly what it said, I wrote it down. 'I'm looking for Harley Jackson. This is Tom Johnson, an attorney based in Portland. I understand you're familiar with Gemma Marlon. We have a question about a legal case pertaining to her and are hoping you might be able to provide some information.'"

Bitter dread coated the insides of my stomach, and I felt a little sick. "Do you recognize that attorney's name?" Daphne pressed.

I swallowed and that familiar panic-laced anxiety tightened around my chest. I took several deep breaths before managing a reply. "I do. Now I have to explain an uncomfortable situation."

"Do you want to meet to talk? Would that be better?"

"Actually, it would. Should we grab coffee at Misty Mountain?"

"I can be there in a half hour," Daphne replied.

––––––––

I took a swallow of coffee, needing the strong flavor. I nervously traced my finger along the edge of the table, wondering when Daphne would arrive. I felt exposed as I sat alone at the table. As if somehow everyone in the café knew my past and the events that left a lingering stain on my life.

Cammi had been sweet as always and had my coffee ready in a jiffy even though she was chatting with another group of customers. Although she hadn't commented, I sensed she noticed I was feeling out of sorts. I didn't know if "out of sorts" could accurately capture how I felt. It was more that an old wash of shame slid through me, followed by a sense of weariness and chaos. I couldn't control the events, and I hated the sense of helplessness.

"Do you want to taste these?" Cammi asked, appearing by the table where I was seated in the corner.

I eyed the tray she held, which had an array of pastries on it. I didn't have much of an appetite, but my body apparently thought otherwise. "Sure," I said, pleased to discover that my voice sounded normal. "What are they?"

"We have several options. I'm doing some menu testing. There are savories—spinach with red peppers and feta, and ham and gruyere popovers. Then, I have sweet options, including apple, blueberry, and elderberry."

"Can I try two?" I asked. Having options made my appetite perk up a little.

"Of course." She handed me a slip of paper. "Let

me know which ones taste the best. I'm actually doing this scientifically." She cast a sheepish grin at that. "Okay, maybe it's not quite scientific, but I want to know what people think."

Glancing down at the paper, I noticed the pastries were listed with space for notes. "I'll try them all." They were small, so that wasn't too much.

"Please do." As she handed me a plate and carefully placed the pastries on it, she asked, "How are you?"

I managed something resembling a smile. "I'm okay. You?"

I mentally congratulated myself for managing a normal conversation even though something weird, stressful, and linked to the most painful part of my life was careening toward me like a meteor I couldn't avoid.

"Busy, but that's life," she replied. "If you need anything, let me know."

Cammi moved on to another table, and moments later, Daphne came through the door to the café. She waved to me before getting in line at the counter. I was hungry enough that I enjoyed the pastries.

Slipping into the chair across from me a few minutes later, Daphne smiled. "Hey, I hear we're testing food."

"I'm a terrible food critic," I offered. "I think they're all good."

"That doesn't make you a terrible food critic," Daphne said reassuringly. "Sometimes they *are* all good."

She looked at the list, her lips curling in a bashful smile. "She's trying my suggestions."

"It's a safe bet that anything you suggest when it comes to food will be good."

Daphne rolled her eyes. "People have different

tastes. We met to discuss what might work here while she's trying to revamp the menu. It's fun to try to help her find things with an original twist and that she can make from local resources when it's in season."

With Daphne's slight southern accent soothing my frayed nerves, we chatted conversationally about the menu, and she made some more detailed notes than what I had to offer on her slip of paper. By the time she brought up my uncomfortable topic, I was relaxed and not feeling so high strung.

"So, tell me what's going on," she said softly. "That message that Harley got was pretty strange."

I took a gulp of coffee. I needed the fortitude of caffeine. After a steadying breath, I began, "It *is* strange. I do know that attorney's name, but not because he's my attorney. He reached out to me as well, asking me to testify on behalf of my old high school softball coach."

Daphne nodded along. "Okay, so what does he want?"

Here came the hard part. No matter how supportive people wanted to be, no one liked to hear uncomfortable stories like this. I had learned, in brutal ways, that some people preferred simply not to know the truth. They preferred for the truth to remain in the shadows and out of sight. Unless it was a truth that was comfortable for them.

"Softball was my big sport in high school. I was really good. We won the state championship twice."

"That's awesome, right?" Daphne asked hesitantly.

"Winning was. What wasn't awesome was that our coach sexually abused some of us. Including me. I never said anything about it until the day I walked in on him with one of my closest friends."

Daphne's eyes widened, and she reached over to

grab my hand. "Oh, no. That's awful. I'm so sorry. What happened after that?"

Daphne exhibited nothing but genuine concern. Relief gusted through me, and I took another breath, her calm and supportive reaction buoying me.

"Well, we decided together to tell our parents, and they went to the school. Everyone on the team was interviewed. A few others came forward, and others didn't. It was pretty ugly. Nothing happened other than that, and he kept on coaching. I lost some friends, including some that surprised me. It was hard for lots of reasons, but also because what bonded us together felt broken." I stumbled over the last word because I didn't like it. It was the only word that rose to the surface when I tried to explain though.

When Daphne nodded encouragingly, I pressed ahead. "My senior year, I actually injured my back and didn't play. I'd always loved riding horses, so I started doing that more. I never competed after that and left the team. He kept coaching, and it all felt like a waste, not worth all the trouble."

Daphne sighed. "I'm so sorry. God, why does it feel like these stories are so similar?"

I shrugged. "Maybe because they are." I didn't even try to keep the bitterness out of my voice. "He went on to get a good job coaching for college teams and led a star team for a few years until there was a case there. Now, things are a little different and people pay more attention. He's facing legal charges for the first time. The DA's office has reached out to me about whether or not I would be willing to testify at his trial to help them establish a pattern of behavior. I'm sure some of my old friends have been asked as well, but I don't know because we haven't stayed in touch. It's been over a decade now."

"What do you want to do?"

"Until his attorney called me, I wasn't sure. That's the attorney who left Harley a message, or that's who I think it is. After he called, I was like fuck this, I'm not going to let them try to manipulate me. Now I'm freaking out though. How does he even know I know Diego, much less Harley? It feels like a nightmare, like they're trying to reach out to people in my life to make me nervous. I came here for a fresh start. My life wasn't ruined. I was doing okay, but the whole situation cast a long shadow. Now, it feels like it's chasing me up here. I wasn't trying to run, but moving on felt good."

Daphne gave my hand a hard squeeze before leaning back in her chair and releasing it. "I know how it feels to have something cast a long shadow. Starting somewhere new isn't running. I can't imagine how it feels to have that attorney reaching out. Things like that happen in high profile cases with attorneys who are getting paid a ton of money. They go looking for any way they can to rattle witnesses. I have no idea how he found out you know Diego, but there's nothing to do about that now."

"I can't even imagine what Diego thinks," I said, leaning my chin in the curve of my palm. "I don't really want to tell him about this. It's not exactly fun to talk about when you're just starting a relationship. I don't even know if I can say we have a relationship."

I meant what I said, but I also knew the way I felt when I was with him. It was much more than a passing, casual encounter. Now my old, ugly history had cast a long line and snagged a hook in my life. Again. The whole situation made me so tired.

Daphne regarded me quietly. "Obviously, I don't know what's in your heart, or Diego's. I do know he likes you an awful lot. Just tell him what happened. You did absolutely nothing wrong. I would also consider contacting an attorney for yourself. If this guy's attorney is going to be reaching out and nosing into people's lives like this, you need someone to make it stop. I would also make sure to let the DA know. They can reach out and help put a stop to it. What a fucking asshole," she said vehemently.

"I don't know if 'asshole' is sufficient for him," I muttered.

"Don't forget you have already moved on from this," she said fiercely. "You're not letting it define your life. Don't let it define your life now."

Daphne's words echoed in my thoughts later. I was *not* going to let the past define my life. Yet, that didn't change how frustrated I was and frankly furious about the actions of that attorney. I was going to take my story back, and I wasn't going to let this man fuck my life up any more than he already had.

Chapter Twenty-Seven

DIEGO

"What do you mean?" Harley pressed, resting a hand on her hip as she cast a skeptical look in Daphne's direction.

Daphne was busy cooking, which she was almost always doing. She seemed to fall into the same kind of zen place I experienced when I was flying whenever she was cooking. For that, I was deeply grateful because her love of cooking benefited my life and that of everyone I cared about immensely.

I waited to hear her response. Unlike my sister, when I was skeptical of a situation, I held back and tried to let things play out. That was really the only way to know the truth.

Daphne turned the burner off under a pan, carefully using the spatula to scoop out the sautéed chicken and place it in a bowl. She glanced over at Harley when she was done, setting the spatula down before looking between us. "It's Gemma's story to tell, and it's personal. I understand why you want to know, especially given that the attorney left you a message.

But it's private. I can assure you Gemma has done nothing nefarious. I suggest you ask her yourself."

Harley let out a huff. "Seriously? You went to talk to her and now you're not going to fill us in."

I felt protective of Gemma, even though doubts were crowding my mind. "Harley, give it a rest. If it's personal, like Daphne said, it's Gemma's story to tell."

Harley narrowed her eyes and looked back at Daphne. "Did Gemma ask you not to tell anyone?"

Daphne rolled her eyes, turning and crossing over to fetch something out of the pantry before returning to the counter. "Not specifically, but it feels like gossip for me to talk about it, and I'm not comfortable with it," Daphne said firmly.

Daphne might not be outwardly as pushy as my sister, but it was obvious she wasn't backing down. Harley tried a few more times to pressure her to no avail.

"Enough. I'll be talking to Gemma tonight because I'm going to her yoga class in town. I'll ask her to give you a call since apparently you can't be bothered to do so yourself," Daphne offered pointedly.

Harley looked at me as if she thought somehow I was going to try to badger Daphne into changing her mind. I shook my head and turned away. I had some laundry to do, which was definitely preferable to getting stuck in the middle of this conversation.

I walked back through the trees to the staff house, relieved to find it empty. For the most part in the summer, there were rarely any of us here at the same time unless it was evening or early morning. We had too many flights rotating in and out to spend much time at home. It was pure chance I had the morning off. The plane I was supposed to be flying today had a minor mechanical issue. Flynn had messaged me about an hour ago to say he'd figured out the issue and the plane would be ready by early afternoon. Until then, I had time on my hands, something I didn't particularly want.

Ever since that strange message Harley received, I felt as if everything had stuttered inside me around Gemma. I couldn't think clearly, and my thoughts were fuzzed with too much emotion and reaction. Striding into my room, I gathered up my laundry and started the washer, promptly realizing that doing the laundry involved a lot of hurry up and wait. This task wasn't going to keep me occupied.

Plunking down on the couch, I decided to peruse the daytime television offerings. Only minutes into that, I was annoyed. My cell phone vibrated from where it sat on the coffee table and I reached for it, answering reflexively without checking the screen to see who was calling.

"Hello?"

"Hello, I'm looking for a Diego Jackson," a man's voice said smoothly.

For a second, I was confused about why I recognized the voice but then I realized this was the voice from Harley's voicemail. Confusion and irritation prickled down my spine, but I decided to roll with it.

"Yes?" I replied

"Is this Mr. Jackson?" the man prompted.

"It is."

"Excellent. I'm calling because I understand you're familiar with a Gemma Marlon."

"Mmm," I replied noncommittally.

"It may seem strange that I'm calling out of the blue. However, I am part of a legal firm in Portland, and Miss Marlon is listed as a witness in an upcoming legal trial. We've had difficulty reaching her, so we're trying to track down people she knows."

"Look, if I knew Gemma, why the hell would I help you? These days that's plain stupid."

"You must understand, she's a witness in a high-profile criminal case involving a famous college coach. We'd like to make sure she's aware of the potential questions should she choose to testify against our client."

"What's this trial about?" I asked, genuinely curious, but also just trying to keep the guy on the phone for a few more minutes.

"You may have heard about it in the news. Our client has been accused of multiple allegations of sexual impropriety with students during his work as a coach. Coaching is his life and his entire career. While we thoroughly respect the efforts to raise the profile of how victims are not served well by the legal system, that doesn't mean everyone accused is guilty. Our country has a legal system and principles for a reason."

My gut churned. I hated stuff like this—when powerful people and those who had enough money could make it difficult for everyone. Although this has absolutely nothing to do with the minor embezzlement case related to my parents, I remembered clearly how much money they had to spend on lawyers to get it addressed legally.

I wasn't about to help this man. "You called the wrong guy. There's no fucking way I'll help you."

I hung up the phone and tossed it on the coffee table, letting out an annoyed sigh. I'd been itching to talk to Gemma. I was going to make it happen and find out just what the hell was going on.

I forced myself to wait until I could switch my laundry over to the dryer before leaving. I could've asked Harley to deal with it, but that required a conversation with her, and she was in a pushy mood.

―――――

"Now, lift your arms, hold your palms flat together, and bend at the waist, coming forward to relax and hang down toward the floor. Please let your knees bend slightly so your lower back can relax. Only straighten your legs if the backs of your thighs are loose enough to do so comfortably."

Gemma's voice rolled over me, soothing and melodic. I followed her instructions, along with the rest of the class, breathing deeply as the tension slowly eased along my spine. When I had checked her class schedule with Daphne and discovered she had a short lunch class, I might've broken a speed record to get into town on time. I had a flight scheduled only an hour away, but I wanted to at least try to talk to Gemma before I left.

We'd done some schedule scrambling with my plane out of commission this morning, so now I was booked for a trip for a group going to Katmai National Park and would be gone for several days.

Gemma brought us through several more poses toward the end of class, and we finished lying flat on our backs with our palms turned upward. Soothing music played as the class slowly filtered apart. Some people hurried out, while I waited.

Gemma seemed tense. Her shoulders were held in a rigid line, and the corners of her eyes were pinched slightly. Her usual easy smile didn't quite reach her eyes. She was chatting with an elderly woman, so I took that moment to grab a bathroom break. When I returned, she was putting away some yoga mats and the music had been turned off. A quick scan around, and I deduced we were finally alone.

Approaching her, I stopped a few feet away. "Gemma."

Her head whipped in my direction quickly, her eyes widening slightly. "Hi, Diego. Good to have you in class." Her tone was polite and crisp.

"Look I was hoping we could talk for a few minutes," I said.

I really didn't want to have this conversation. I wanted there to be no confusing mystery about why an attorney was calling people Gemma knew. My gut told me there was a reason they had targeted Harley and me. If only because we were new enough in Gemma's world that we might be susceptible to revealing information about Gemma without her knowledge.

Gemma's eyes searched my face, her gaze guarded. "Sure, what is it?"

"You heard about the message that attorney left Harley?"

She nodded. "Daphne spoke to me about it. Please let Harley know I'm sorry. Obviously, I had nothing to do with that. Well, I have something to do with the situation, but not having some random attorney call people I don't know that well."

"You know *me* well," I heard myself saying.

She regarded me quietly. "I think so," she said, her words hesitant.

"Tell me what happened."

Her lips pressed in a thin line, and she looked away. She pointlessly straightened a few of the rolled up yoga mats on the shelf. "It's a long story, and not really the kind of story I want to tell a guy who I'm still getting to know."

When she looked back toward me, her gaze was

steady. She lifted her chin slightly and crossed her arms in front of her chest. "I'm guessing Harley's a little freaked out about that message."

I shrugged. "It was out of the blue for her, and she didn't really understand it, but I don't think she's freaking out. Daphne told us it was personal."

Gemma looked torn, her lips twisting to the side. "I didn't ask her to keep anything secret."

"She said that you didn't, but she felt it was your story to tell. Tell me. I suppose I should let you know that same attorney called me today."

Her eyes flew wide, her breath hissing with a surprised inhalation. "What? What did he want?"

"He said something about making sure that you understood it was a serious matter and that they were having trouble getting a hold of you. My gut tells me he's an asshole."

Her arms tightened, and she curled her hands around the sides of her waist and turned away from me. When she looked back in my direction, she looked weary and sad. "I used to play competitive softball in high school. We were a championship team." Her tone was thoughtful, almost detached. "It all blew up when our coach kissed me and tried to take things a little further. Don't worry, he didn't rape me," she added hurriedly.

Anger bolted through me hard and fast, but I gritted my teeth and stayed silent.

"It wasn't just me. I wasn't special. Not that I felt special. I didn't want to feel special, and I didn't want him to ever look at me again. It happened to some of my teammates who were my friends. They investigated, but then nothing. The school did their own investigation," she said with air quotes around investigation. "I moved on with my life and actually injured my back at the start of the following season. We were all pretending like it was no big deal. I guess we thought that's what we were supposed to do since the investigation went nowhere. Fast forward, and he went on to be a championship winning coach for more than one college and now he's finally facing criminal charges. I wasn't sure if I was going to testify, but now I am. My brother thinks he's trying to search out people close to me to scare me out of testifying."

"Are you fucking kidding me?!" I finally burst out.

Gemma turned to me, her gaze unsettlingly calm. "Of course not. You just told me he called you too. I have a message in to my brother. He's an attorney. I'm hoping he can tell the coach's attorneys to back the fuck off and leave me alone. Because I *will* be testifying."

She fell completely silent for a moment. The thud of my heartbeat echoed in my ears. With her arms still tightly wrapped around her waist, she turned away and walked to the windows at the front of the room. I followed her over, as if she had a string attached to me.

"So, that's a fun thing to learn about the girl you only had two dinners with," she said, her words sharp like pieces of glass.

"Gemma, I know life's not all fun. I'm really, *really* sorry you went through that."

My words felt pathetically inadequate.

She finally let her arms drop free, lifting one hand to rub at the back of her neck before spinning away. "It's life. We all have shit we go through. I actually need to get going."

She hurried into a small room off the main room, returning with her purse and slipping into a light-weight jacket as she stuffed her feet into a pair of tennis shoes. I didn't know why, but it felt as if she were slipping away from me.

"Gemma," I began

She shook her head. "You can't fix this, Diego. Please let Harley know I'm sorry that attorney called her. I have no idea how they got your number or hers. I'll let you know what my brother says."

She moved so fast she was already at the front door before I caught up to her. "When can I see you again?" I asked.

Her eyes lifted to mine, but they were shuttered, closed off to me. "I'm sure I'll see you when I come out for a yoga class at the resort. I'll be there tomorrow night."

"I'm leaving for a three-day trip over in Katmai, so I won't see you there."

"Then, next week," she said brightly, her smile almost brittle.

She was already stepping through the door, holding it for me. I waited while she locked up behind us. "How about this weekend?" I pressed. "I'll be back by then."

"I'm busy," she said tightly. "Go on your trip, and I'll see you next week at the resort."

She didn't give me a chance to debate further, lifting her hand in a wave and almost running to her car.

I stood where I was, watching as she drove away and wondering just how I'd gotten this so wrong.

Chapter Twenty-Eight

DIEGO

I was cutting it close by the time I arrived at the plane hangar and hustled to get the plane ready for the trip. "Thanks, man," I called over to Ryan Brooks.

Ryan was a young guy who was working on getting his pilot's license and also doing side work as a mechanic. Flynn had been hiring him for small repair jobs. While all of us could handle repairs, we were busy enough as it was. He grinned in my direction. "Anytime. You guys keep me busy and are great references for me."

Ryan was the younger brother of Eli Brooks, a friend who owned a local guiding and outdoor shop. Having Ryan work for us was a mutually beneficial arrangement. We sent customers to Eli, and Ryan logged plenty of those flight training hours. Flynn insisted on paying him his full rate for mechanic work, even though Ryan was always trying to give us a discount.

He did us a solid by squeezing us in on short notice whenever he could as he'd done this morning. Before he'd even driven away, a car pulled up in the parking area, and a family poured out of it. The distraction I needed so desperately was here in the form of two teenage boys who helped me load up the plane. Their parents were patient with them, and the family was beyond excited to go on this trip into the wilderness.

While they waited to board, I ran into the hangar for a last check to grab my gear bag and make sure I had a fully charged radio and a backup battery. My cell phone buzzed as I was walking out of the restroom. Seeing Harley's name on the screen, I answered quickly, "What's up, Sis? I've only got a minute because I'm about to fly."

"Oh, that's right. I forgot you're gone for three days. Well, that attorney called me. Again." She proceeded to repeat some variation of what the attorney had said to me, but added, "He said Gemma could be in real trouble if she doesn't get in touch with them."

I wanted to scream in frustration. Gemma had given me the rundown, but I didn't like how Harley was getting caught up in this. My sister who never wanted to be told to back down was going to have to fucking back down.

"Harley, leave it alone, okay? I talked to Gemma today. She hasn't done anything wrong. The smartest thing for you to do is not to take those calls. Those people are trying to fuck with her."

"Well, maybe if you would let me know what the hell was going on—"

I cut her off quickly. "Daphne was right. It's personal, and it's up to Gemma to tell whoever she wants to tell. You're my sister, and I love you, but you need to trust me on this."

I hung up the phone, hoping and praying Harley would take my words to heart. Unsure what my options were considering that I had a professional obligation and needed to leave, I pulled Gemma's name up and sent her a quick text.

Just a heads up. That attorney spoke to Harley again. I didn't tell her what you shared with me because that's your call. Maybe you better get a hold of your brother sooner rather than later.

My thumbs hovered over the screen. They actually itched to type out the words "I love you." Which was fucking insane. What the hell was I thinking? I was getting *way* ahead of myself.

I'll be back in three days. I'll be thinking of you. If you need anything from me, call Daphne. Flynn can reach me. Please take care of yourself and please call your brother.

Chapter Twenty-Nine

GEMMA

The phone rang in my ear, the sound jangling along the edges of my already frayed nerves. Just when I thought I was going to get my brother's voicemail, he answered.

"Hey, Gemma. What's up?" Neal asked.

I took a shallow breath, swallowing nervously before I could explain. My pause must've dragged too long because Neal prompted, "Gemma?"

"Hey," I finally managed, my voice sounding bright and kind of normal. "Look, I need help. Some weird stuff has happened."

I quickly explained the situation. As I spoke, I was surprised at how ridiculous the whole thing sounded. I couldn't believe my former coach had hired a law firm that would actually try to interfere in my personal life for the sole purpose of trying to intimidate me from testifying.

Neal, on the other hand, didn't seem rattled at all. "It's par for the course, Gemma. You've seen the news. The easiest way to get people to shut up is to make them uncomfortable about it. Don't worry. I'll handle it. We can file a cease and desist order, and we can also put some pretty heavy pressure on them from the DA. Courts don't appreciate attempts to interfere with witnesses. I don't know if this rises to obstruction, but it's possible. I'm going to guess you're not the only potential witness they've reached out to."

"But why call my friends? Not to mention, I just started seeing this guy. It feels like they're spying on me. It's really creepy."

"That's the point," he said dryly. "To make you uncomfortable. I'm guessing they hired a private investigator who somehow figured out you went on a few dates with this guy. Somebody new in your life is easier to influence than someone who's known you for a long time. This guy didn't know anything about the case, right?"

"No! It's not exactly a great getting-to-know-you topic. So, I get an investigator finding out I've gone on a few dates with him and calling him and his sister. That just feels so invasive. I'm mortified."

"That's the exact point. I'll deal with this. They *will* back off. I promise," Neal said firmly. "Have you talked to Mom and Dad about this?"

"Ugh. No. Why would I want to do that? As it is, I'm already our family's hot mess. I really prefer not to involve them in everything, Neal. I know you probably don't understand that."

My brother was quiet, and I heard his sigh filter through the phone line. "I do get it, Gemma. You're not our family's hot mess, and I wish you wouldn't describe yourself like that. Mom and Dad just want to be there for you."

"I'll call Mom today. I should also let you know I've decided to testify. I have a message in to the DA's office."

"It's totally your choice. Remember that."

"I will."

"I've got a call coming in, so I need to go. Love you," Neal said.

"Love you too."

I hung up the phone, wondering what to do next. Feeling betwixt and between with anxiety twisting inside me, I decided to go for a ride. Charlie could use the exercise, and I needed to do something that would help me relax. I was heading out to the resort for my two classes there this evening, and I had plenty of time for a ride before that.

———

"Please hold," the receptionist said politely in my ear.

The man seemed oblivious to my distress. What was probably a routine for him had my heart pounding in an unsteady beat in my chest and my breath coming short. It wasn't excitement, it was raw anxiety revving my body's engine. I managed to take a slow breath, the tension churning inside easing, but just barely.

"Hello, Gemma?" a woman's voice said.

"Yes, this is Gemma." My words came out fast, bumping into each other.

"Very good to hear from you. I should let you know, I've already spoken to your brother today. I'm very sorry to hear about Mr. Johnson. I don't know if this will help you feel better, but they've done something similar to several witnesses. It's dirty tricks and it's not okay. We will be notifying the court. You can be prepared for the defendant to claim he had no idea his attorneys were doing it, but we'll deal with that."

For the first time, my brother's tendency to be on top of things and always timely sent a whoosh of relief through me. When I was younger, I used to get annoyed with how prompt he was. My struggles with dyslexia had me fumbling in school until we figured out what the problem was. Delaying and avoiding things had been a go-to coping skill of mine when I was younger. That was the very opposite of my brother. I was much better about things now, but still. Sibling relationships were the scaffolding of childhood frustrations even when you loved each other.

"Now, how can I help you?" the attorney's question brought me back to the conversation at hand.

"I'm calling because I've decided I'd like to testify. I was getting to that decision anyway, but having that attorney call me and then my friends, pushed me over the edge. I'm angry."

Although the DA couldn't see me, I straightened my shoulders as I stared out over the view through the windows. The mountains stood sentry in the distance, tall and quiet, their commanding presence giving me a dose of strength.

Although I was weary of the threat of this trauma running through my life, for the first time it felt like I was taking the reins of the narrative. Maybe, just maybe, this would help me finally stop sidestepping it.

"I'm glad to hear it," she said warmly. "Obviously, we never want to pressure people to testify. I can only imagine how it felt for you when the original case went absolutely nowhere. You will not be alone in this process, and I hope it might give you some closure. It will certainly bolster our case. I'd like you to know we have a very strong case against the coach. With or without your testimony and that of other supporting witnesses, I think he will finally face genuine legal consequences."

"I hope so," I whispered. "I really hope so."

Our conversation shifted into her explanation of the process and how she would set up an interview for me via videoconference with one of her staff to review what my testimony would cover and to support me.

I hung up a little while later, feeling strong and shaky. I was ready to face this down. But first, I had a life—a life here in Alaska and yoga classes to teach. I left my house, heading out to Walker Adventures, wishing Diego would be there tonight.

Chapter Thirty

DIEGO

I leaned against the railing on a viewing platform at Brooks Falls in Katmai National Park, watching the brown bears feed on the salmon that came through the river here every year. It was still awe inspiring even though I'd been here several times a year since I'd moved to Alaska.

It blew my mind to watch the majestic and decidedly massive bears snatch fresh salmon out of the stream. As nature's bounty went, this was clearly a prime restaurant in brown bear world. We were on our second day there, and the weather had been fantastic for the family who booked this trip. There were clear skies with fluffy clouds occasionally scudding against the bright blue backdrop. The good weather didn't negate the mosquitoes though, and one buzzed incessantly near my ear. I swatted futilely at it. Like many things, even the mosquitoes took being Alaskan to heart. They were so large they looked like the insect version of weight lifters.

"Hey, Diego," a voice said.

Glancing over my shoulder, I saw Natalie Taylor approaching. Her dark hair was tucked under a baseball cap, and she waved as she got closer. "Hey," I replied. "What are you doing here?"

She grinned when she stopped beside me. "Probably the same thing you are. I might not have flown the plane, but I'm guiding a group on some hikes here. I came up with Lacey's adventure outfit."

I knew Lacey Haynes from Diamond Creek. Natalie lived in Anchorage and picked up outdoor guiding jobs all over Alaska. Lacey and her husband, Quinn, ran a small company that handled outdoor trips all over Alaska. Quinn didn't do much guiding himself, seeing as he was the primary doctor at a local medical office. Lacey ran a few, but she also hired lots of people seasonally to help when she wasn't able to do the guiding herself.

Natalie's brown eyes twinkled as she looked up at me, and I didn't miss the teasing glint there. We had had a few encounters, for lack of a better way to describe it. Perhaps occasional friends with occasional benefits was what we were. She wasn't around enough for me to consider her a close friend.

"You here for the night?" she asked.

"I am. We fly out first thing tomorrow. You?"

"Just got here today. Guess my timing was better than I expected."

I shrugged noncommittally, relieved when there was a nearby commotion. Glancing over, I saw that a group of younger guests had gotten a little too close for comfort and a bear had lunged in the tall grass nearby. The kids were smart enough to immediately respond and take a few steps away from the railing.

"Bears are going to be bear," Natalie said lightly. "So, what's been going on for you?"

"Not much new. I fly, and I love my freaking job. It's our busy season, so I don't have much downtime. You doing any other trips for Lacey and Quinn this summer?"

"I signed up to cover three. I should be in Diamond Creek for a few weeks. Maybe after tonight we could actually see each other again."

I silently groaned. She had expectations. I couldn't say I blamed her for them. Now that I contemplated it, the last few times I'd seen her, which had been less than once a year, we had enjoyed each other's company, intimately speaking.

While I might not have been certain about my feelings for Gemma before, they became blindingly clear in this moment. I had absolutely zero interest in Natalie, or any other woman. Gemma was the one and only woman I wanted. I figured I might as well face this head-on instead of trying to sidestep the topic. With us being here tonight and not much else going on, I didn't want to be coy about it.

"Look," I began, "I'm seeing someone. It's great to see you, but—"

She cut in quickly. "I've been officially friend zoned. Got it." She nodded firmly. "I appreciate you being direct about it."

I experienced a twinge of discomfort. "Friend zoned? I didn't know we were ever more than friends."

"We weren't. You don't need to explain. But you just explicitly told me we *won't* be anything more. I didn't think we were more than friends, but we did cross the just-friends boundary a few times," she explained.

I opened my mouth to press the issue. "I never meant to lead you on."

Natalie rolled her eyes. "I know you didn't, but a

girl can hope. We had fun. I'm also a sucker for unattainable men. The worst is when someone unattainable becomes attainable for somebody else."

"Hey," I began, only to shut up right quick when she shook her head sharply.

"For God's sake, don't apologize. You must like this girl. Is it serious?"

I was nodding before I even formulated my answer. Maybe we had only had two official dates, but so much more had passed between Gemma and me. Just thinking about her now led to a shaft of fierce longing. I wished I was back in Diamond Creek. I hadn't liked leaving with everything so unsettled. I hoped Gemma was doing okay and that my sister had enough sense not to make more trouble than was necessary.

"Good. If you're gonna fall, I want it to be worth it."

I chuckled. "It is. Here's hoping I don't screw anything up."

"Don't forget to tell her how much she means to you. That's pretty key," Natalie offered helpfully.

———

The following morning dawned cool and so foggy we couldn't even see the sky. The fog was a thick mist, draped over everything like a dense blanket. Normally, I was good at rolling with the weather. That was part of being a pilot in the wilderness of Alaska. The weather dictated everything. In this case, it meant me searching out the family I was supposed to be flying back to Diamond Creek this morning.

"We're not going anywhere yet," I said to the father. "This might burn off this afternoon, but we need it to burn off in time for us to get up in the air and back. I'm going to check in with the staff here and find out what the weather report is. I'll also radio out to the resort. They'll have an update too. Best part, you guys can get some more free views. I hope you didn't have anything too expensive scheduled for tomorrow back across the bay."

The mother grinned. "We knew the weather might affect timing, so we made sure to leave two days open on either side of this trip."

"Smart plan," I replied. "Stay close, so I can find you easily if the sun breaks through this fog."

I headed back toward the plane to radio over to Flynn. A few minutes later, I had Flynn on the line. "For the moment, we're fogged in."

"Figured I'd be hearing from you soon," he replied. "On this side, you might be socked in for another day or two. There's a rain system crossing through. It's not supposed to clear up until tomorrow afternoon. I think that'll be too late for you to leave."

"Fuck," I muttered.

"What's wrong? You usually roll with the weather."

"I know, but I'm worried about Gemma. Do you have any news?"

"I'll check with Daphne. Harley cooled her heels."

"Thank God for small favors," I replied with a chuckle.

"Have any messages you want me to pass along? I'm sure I could get a message to Gemma," Flynn offered.

All I wanted was to see Gemma. I didn't want to be passing along a message through a friend about how I felt. Not now. "Hopefully I'll be back tomorrow, and maybe the weather report's wrong."

Flynn barked a laugh at that. "Right. It's usually only wrong when the weather's supposed to be nice," he said dryly.

I sighed. "A guy can hope."

Chapter Thirty-One

GEMMA

"Yes!" Cat declared as she came running out of the ocean water dragging a net behind her.

I stood on the sand, damp from the rhythmic roll of the waves breaking onto the shoreline by the river that flowed in from the ocean. Dipnetting was an activity I'd never witnessed and a sight to behold.

Cat swiped her braid off her shoulder as she grinned up at me while she untangled the salmon from the gillnet. With quick, efficient moves, she clubbed the fish and only moments later gutted it. Gulls were calling raucously in the air above us. One swooped down to pick up the fish waste.

I'd met Nora in town early this morning to go with her and Cat to the mouth of the Kenai River, north of Diamond Creek. The shoreline was getting more crowded by the minute with new people arriving with coolers, many fully dressed in hip waders, and some in wetsuits. They stood in the icy cold waters with long handled nets to catch the salmon that were racing up the river to spawn.

Since I was a new resident in Alaska, I could only

watch. Cat had explained the dipnetting regulations and process on the drive up. She'd put me in charge of the cooler once she and Nora were ready to go in the water. I poured fresh ice over the next fish she placed in there, watching as she ran back into the water immediately.

Roughly an hour later, Nora grinned over at me as she sprayed a hose on her boots and waders in the parking area. "Wow, today was quick. We got our limit inside of three hours."

Everything had happened so quickly this morning, I was having trouble keeping up. "I can't believe you have forty-five fish in those coolers." Aside from being in charge of the coolers, I'd also been put in charge of the count. At first, I'd thought we were talking about maybe ten fish, but then I realized I actually needed to keep track unless I wanted to be pawing through slippery fish after the fact to count them. I'd used my phone to jot down the rapid increase until they reached their total.

Nora chuckled. "It seems like a lot, but we'll eat it all this coming winter. Me, Flynn and Cat count as a household. You can get twenty-five salmon for the head of the household, and ten more for each additional member. The guys in the staff house count as a separate household, but they're coming up another day."

With Diego across the bay, and me feeling unsettled and worried about our last conversation, I'd been relieved when Nora had texted to invite me along on this jaunt. I couldn't say I'd completely banished Diego from my thoughts today, but he hadn't loomed as large as he had lately. The day was simply too busy with activity and the scents and sounds of the ocean and the birds calling. I'd even watched an eagle land on the shore to snatch a fish from someone only moments after they brought it ashore.

"This is the craziest thing I've ever seen. I thought salmon was a big deal in Seattle and Portland," I commented.

Cat stopped beside me, her smile wide. "I love dipnetting. It's my favorite thing every year. Next year, you'll get to do it."

"Can we plan ahead for me to come with you all?" I asked.

Nora nodded as she tossed her now rinsed gear in an empty bin in the back of one of the resort trucks. "Of course. It's fun no matter what, but it's more fun together, and it helps to have extra hands. We ready to roll?" Her gaze shifted to Cat.

"Yep. Let's get some fresh ice at the convenience store on the way out," Cat replied.

Once we were in the truck and driving back toward Diamond Creek and the mad rush of the morning receded, Diego came strolling into my thoughts again. I felt twisted up inside over him.

Cat was driving because she got her license, apparently only days prior. She'd explained to me this morning that this was their only automatic truck. Even though she knew how to drive a stick shift, she was more comfortable driving an automatic.

Nora turned sideways in the seat in front of me, hooking her arm over the back of it. "So, how are things with Diego?"

I heard myself confiding before I had even considered it. "I don't know. I'm guessing because Harley is the type of person to talk that you probably heard about those weird calls."

Cat glanced over her shoulder, smiling sympathetically. "It'll be fine. Diego *really* likes you."

"Keep your eyes on the road," Nora prompted warmly.

Cat obeyed, and Nora cast a smile at me. "Diego does really like you. He's a great guy."

"I know he is," I said, my heart aching a little in my chest. "I feel like I kind of screwed up. It wasn't a big deal, but he tried to talk to me, and I blew him off."

Nora's brown eyes regarded me warmly. "You can talk to him the next time you get a chance."

Cat snorted in the seat beside her.

"What?" Nora asked.

"It's just funny to hear you telling someone to talk. You haven't talked to Gabriel for weeks now."

Nora actually growled at her sister, and I couldn't help the laugh that escaped.

"How about you stay out of my business?" Nora returned, not even noticing my unintended laugh.

"Never," Cat countered quickly.

When Nora looked back at me, I took pity on her. "Siblings. It's a thing. I get it. I have a brother. It gets better when you're older."

Cat kept her eyes on the road and called back to me, "Does it? Because I have three older siblings, and they all have an opinion on everything I do."

Nora cuffed her lightly on the shoulder. "It's because we love you."

"Exactly why I think you should talk to Gabriel," Cat replied.

This time, Nora sighed and looked back toward me with a shrug. "Maybe I'm no expert, but Cat's right, Diego really likes you. Whether I follow my own advice or not, you should talk to him when he gets back."

I looked pointlessly at the clock mounted on the wall at the yoga studio. Class had finished only moments ago, so I knew perfectly well it was a few minutes past six. Glancing out the windows, I sighed. I was alone in the studio as I tidied up. The sky was foggy and a steady drizzle had been falling all afternoon.

Although I wasn't a pilot, I had enough sense to know it was highly unlikely Diego had flown back to Diamond Creek today as planned. That knowledge didn't change how much I wanted to see him. It added a layer of worry to the jumble of emotions tangling inside me.

On the way home, I checked in with my parents and my brother. My mother had taken the news about my choice to testify with calm support. I suspected my brother had told her to stop jabbering on about how "freeing" it would be for me. My dad wasn't much of a phone person, but he hopped on the line to tell me he loved me. It was strange, but all my anxiety about testifying had eased. Something about the process of actually preparing to do it helped. I was doing something concrete instead of merely worrying about it. I also hadn't heard another word from that attorney. I laughed to myself when I thought about that because Harley had apparently told them off and called me to make sure I knew.

I headed home that evening and decided to take an evening ride with Charlie. I was growing to love the long summer days because I had more hours after the end of my workday to spend with the horses and do other things.

"Hey, bud," I said, patting his neck lightly once I was situated in the saddle.

I adjusted the reins in my hands and gave him a light tap with my heels. Ever since the incident where he'd tossed me off, I stuck strictly to riding in the pasture. I'd set up a few rails to trot over and a small jump.

After a few minutes of walking and practicing halting and turning, we set off at an easy trot. I took a breath, savoring the spruce scented air and his comfortable gait. Charlie was a great horse and had the most comfortable trot. I posted in an easy rhythm as we circled along the fence. After several passes over the rails, I decided to try the jump.

"Let's do this," I murmured to Charlie as I gathered the reins a little more firmly in my hands.

He cleared the low jump smoothly. "Good boy." I patted him on the neck and circled back for another jump.

This time, he came to a jerking stop, so hard that I tumbled over his neck, landing right on the jump. "Oof!"

Piercing pain radiated from my elbow, which had landed against the railing. Not that it was very high off the ground, a foot if that.

I stayed still and took stock. My hip was throbbing and my elbow hurt like hell, but otherwise I felt fine. Charlie stood exactly where he stopped, staring down at me curiously as if he couldn't figure out how I'd ended up there in front of him.

I moved carefully and climbed to my feet. "Well, I guess we weren't ready for more than one jump," I murmured to him.

He snorted and nudged my hip. I was wearing my riding pants, rather than my jeans where I usually had treats in my pocket. "We're gonna have to get back to the barn for a treat."

I limped back into the barn with him, a little concerned about my elbow. Although it throbbed, I made sure to get his tack taken off and brushed him down before putting him in his stall. I decided to feed the horses an early dinner and call it a night. I didn't think I was up for coming back to let them out.

When I was in the shower a short while later, I glanced down to my hip to see a bruise already forming and inspected my elbow. It was bruised as well, but I hoped that was the worst of it.

I woke the following day, uncomfortably sore. I thought my hip was going to be okay despite the nasty bruise, but my elbow had swollen more during the night. I was going to need to call off my yoga classes and visit the doctor.

Chapter Thirty-Two

DIEGO

I stared at the note taped on the door at Gemma's yoga studio. "Classes are canceled for today. Thank you for your understanding."

What the fuck was going on? Worry stormed through me. Gemma hadn't replied to the text I sent after I landed and no one seemed to know where she was.

This wasn't like her. Returning to my truck, I tapped the screen to call Daphne as soon as I was driving. "Have you heard from Gemma?"

"Uh, no," Daphne said slowly. "I didn't even know you were back yet."

"I landed a half an hour ago. I went to find Gemma at her yoga studio because I figured she had an evening class, but there's a note on the door saying classes are canceled."

"Have you tried calling her?" Daphne asked helpfully.

"Obviously, I tried calling her. That's why I'm calling you."

Daphne was quiet for a few beats before offering,

"I'm not sure who else to call. She lives alone. Maybe go check out at her house. I'll try to call her too."

I didn't like this, not at all. Aiming my truck toward her place, I drove faster than I should to get there. Her car wasn't there, and the house was locked. The horses eyed me from the pasture.

I paused to greet them, all of them hanging their heads over the fence for me to pet them. "Don't suppose y'all know where she is," I murmured.

I felt unsettled and didn't want to drive all the way out to the resort until I knew where Gemma was. I pulled my phone out, calling again. I got her voicemail. Again.

"Gemma, it's Diego. I tried to catch you at your yoga studio, but it says classes are canceled. I'm just checking to see if you're okay."

Chapter Thirty-Three

GEMMA

"It's sprained?" I asked the friendly doctor.

The doctor, who insisted I call him Quinn, nodded. "Yep. That's why the swelling's so bad. You'll be fine, but this kind of sprain actually takes as long to heal as a bone break."

"You're kidding," I sputtered, glancing down at the offending elbow.

Quinn chuckled. "The elbow's a busy joint. Fortunately, it's not weight bearing. You'll need to keep it stable in a sling for a few weeks. I'll give you some exercises to do. You're the new yoga teacher in town, right?"

He spun on his stool, opening a cabinet door beside the counter. He stood to reach something higher on the shelf, bringing down a sling packaged in plastic. "Let's see if this one fits."

"I'm the yoga teacher," I offered with a smile when he faced me again. "I had to cancel my classes today because this was bothering me too much. I guess I'll be teaching in a sling for a little while."

"That'll be perfectly fine. You can do yoga with one arm and two legs," he replied with a wry smile.

"Dr. Haynes—" I began

He shook his head and tapped his hand on his name badge, which said Quinn Haynes, M.D.

"Call me Quinn. This is a small town and I run the only family practice here. I *am* your doctor, but it feels strange to stand on ceremony when I'm also going to see you in the grocery store and maybe even out for a drink sometime."

I smiled, emotion welling inside. I was starting to feel like I belonged here, like I might be someone he saw and knew in the grocery store. I didn't want to burst into happy tears in my new doctor's office, so I took a breath.

"Quinn, I really need my elbow to get better. I can deal with the yoga limitations, but I also take care of four horses."

"Ah, you're the person who rented Claire's old place. I heard she's thinking of selling."

"Really?" I was completely derailed by this topic and barely noticed as Quinn expertly fit the sling on my elbow.

"That's the word. My wife's mother knows everything and is close with her. They stay in touch via text, email, and phone. It's a great piece of property. If you like the horses, maybe you should call her."

Our conversation was cut off by a nurse popping in to let Quinn know they had a new patient, a little boy who apparently had a fish hook in his hand.

Quinn glanced my way after adjusting the sling. "Off to the next patient. I think you're all set. The main thing is to be careful and not overdo it with this arm. Check in with my receptionist and make sure to schedule a follow-up appointment in a few weeks.

Otherwise, it was great to meet you. Perhaps, I'll find some time to get to your yoga class soon."

He rushed off, and I did as instructed and scheduled my next appointment. On the way out, I met Quinn's wife, Lacey, although I didn't know who she was at first. She stopped me in the parking lot.

"Hey," she said enthusiastically. "You're the yoga teacher, right?"

"I am." I paused, unsure what to say to the woman approaching me.

"I'm Lacey Haynes." She paused, glancing to my arm in its sling. "Are you okay?"

"Mostly. I sprained my elbow. If I have it right, you're Quinn's wife," I said hesitantly.

"You got it." Lacey had a warm, tomboyish quality to her with chestnut hair and pretty green eyes. "I'm coming to your class with my sister next week. I've been meaning to come sooner, but you know how life is."

"I do. Life often gets in the way," I replied. "It's nice to meet you. By the way, I'm Gemma Marlon."

"So nice to meet you. I'm sorry about your elbow."

I rolled my eyes. "It's a minor sprain, but hopefully it will heal quickly."

"You're in good hands with Quinn. Will you still teach classes?"

"Oh, yes. I don't need my elbow to teach class," I said with a soft laugh.

"By the way, Diego should be back soon," Lacey added.

She must've seen the confusion on my face and clarified. "You're seeing him, right?"

Uncertain how to respond, I nodded if only because I wanted her to continue.

"I run an expedition program, and we sent a group

over to Katmai. The weather kept everybody behind, but I heard this morning that he was flying back." There was a vibrating sound, and Lacey slipped her phone out of her pocket. Glancing at the screen, she added, "I need to take this. Great to meet you and I'll see you soon." She hurried off with a wave.

I climbed into my car, my mind caught on another loop of Diego. I'd been trying not to think too much about him. *Trying* being the operative word. I was utterly failing.

I wished I didn't miss him. It seemed ridiculous to miss him. He'd only been gone for a few days now. I felt like I'd screwed up our last conversation, and I didn't know how to fix it. Diego was the first man who made me wish I didn't have the stain on my past. Because what man would want to be with a woman whose first kisses were with her coach?

I knew, I *knew*, that thinking that way about it didn't make sense. It wasn't my fault. And yet, I had internalized the idea that it was. That's what happened when you tried to get help and absolutely nothing happened.

Chapter Thirty-Four

DIEGO

I was more than ready for a hot shower and a change of clothes. I told myself it didn't make sense to try to see Gemma right away. She'd made it clear she didn't want to see me. And she hadn't responded to my message.

Apparently, my hands had other ideas. As soon as my truck came close to the road that led to her place, I turned. Mentally, I asked myself why, but I kept going.

When I pulled in, I didn't have a plan. Then, I saw Gemma walking into the barn with her arm in a sling. What the hell?

She didn't look back, and I presumed she hadn't heard me pulling in. I hustled out of my truck and jogged across the parking area, following her into the barn. I saw her just as she turned into the feed room at the back. In another second, I was standing in the doorway.

"What happened?"

Gemma spun around quickly, her eyes wide. "Diego, what are you doing here?"

I crossed the dusty floor to her, glancing down to her arm, cradled against the front of her body with a royal blue sling.

"What happened?" I repeated.

She let out a soft sigh and rolled her eyes. "I fell. I knew better, but Charlie was doing great. It's not a big deal. I just sprained my elbow. Quinn thinks I must've twisted it a little bit when I landed."

"Does it hurt?"

"It's sore, but with the sling, it's pretty comfortable. Ibuprofen is enough to knock the edge off the pain." She paused, her eyes searching mine. "How was your trip? I heard the weather held you up."

I was distracted and had to mentally jerk my attention to her question. "Did you get my message?"

She looked puzzled. She slipped her phone out of her pocket and tapped the screen open. "Ah, I missed the call and didn't even check to see if I had any messages. Should I play it?"

"No need. I was wondering if you were okay. That's all."

"How was your trip?" she prompted again.

"It was fine. The weather was nice for two days, and then we woke up to heavy fog and drizzle the day we were supposed to leave."

We stared at each other quietly, and the space around us felt crowded with emotions. I didn't want to push, but I *did* want her to know how I felt. I recalled Natalie's advice. *"Don't forget to tell her how much she means to you. That's pretty key."*

"Look, I know the timing isn't great, but I want you to know I'm falling for you—big-time. I get it if you're not in the same place, but I wanted you to know how I felt."

Gemma's mouth fell open and her breath hissed

through her teeth when she drew it in sharply. When she blinked rapidly, I realized her eyes were filling with tears.

"Oh, fuck. I didn't mean to make you cry."

I moved to embrace her, and a sense of relief and rightness rolled through me as I folded her into my arms. I moved carefully, making sure not to jostle her arm. She was soft and warm, and she tucked her head into the curve of my neck. I breathed in her scent and savored the feel of having her back in my arms.

She murmured something into my chest. "What was that, sugar?"

She lifted her head, her eyes glittering as she peered up at me. "I'm falling for you too. Big time."

Vulnerability flickered in her gaze, while my heart kicked hard against my ribs and I found it hard to catch my breath. I slid my hand up her back, lightly cupping her nape as I dipped my head and brushed my lips across hers. Electricity sizzled where we connected, but I checked the urge to dive into a deep, hard kiss.

"Well, that's a relief," I murmured when I lifted my head, my lips twitching with a smile.

We stood there staring at each other in the quiet room. The sound of one of the horses neighing came from a distance, and a magpie chattered outside the barn. A shaft of sunlight fell through the window, illuminating the dust motes floating in the air.

Gemma's lips curled in a slow smile. "That was a long four days," she whispered.

"Yeah?"

A lock of hair fell over her eyes as she nodded, and I lifted a hand to brush it away, tucking it behind her ear. Then, we were kissing, tumbling into one kiss after another. I lost sight of everything but the feel of her tongue gliding against mine, the soft give of her lips, and the little sounds that came from the back of her throat.

Every sensation spun into the storm of need and emotion inside. The only thing that snapped me out of it was when I moved to bring her closer against me and felt her sling.

I abruptly lifted my head. "Fuck. I forgot about your arm. Are you okay?"

Gemma stared back at me, her eyes dark and her lips puffy from our kisses. "Yes. That's what the sling is for. I can hardly move my arm in it." She cocked her head to the side. "Don't tell me this means you're gonna stop this."

Feeling flustered, an emotion with which I was not particularly familiar, I stepped a little further back, needing the space between us to think clearly. "Gemma, you're injured."

Her lips narrowed in a line. "It's my elbow, and it's just a sprain. We can make this work."

"Let's finish taking care of the horses first," I hedged.

Gemma let out a long sigh. "Fine. That's why I'm out here anyway."

Relieved, I followed her and quickly helped to get the hay and feed taken care of for the horses. She got annoyed with me when I insisted on handling all the hay.

"I can get that, you know," she protested.

I gave her a long look. "I know you can. But when I have two arms to use, there's no sense in making you go to the trouble to handle these bales with only one."

She rolled her eyes and went to let the horses in. A few minutes later, we were standing in her kitchen.

Her eyes coasted over me. "Tell me more about your trip."

I shrugged. "There's not much to tell. The view was great, and the family who booked the trip had a great time watching bears. It was fine until we got fogged in. I was impatient to get back."

Gemma's eyes dropped, and she traced her finger around an empty glass sitting on the counter. When her lashes swept up, she looked pained. "I'm sorry."

"For what?"

"I kind of freaked out and pushed you away before you left."

"It's okay. Really. You were dealing with some hard stuff."

We were standing only about a foot apart, and I reached for her again. I needed to feel her, to have the tactile experience of holding her.

She came easily, tucking her chin into the curve of my neck. I trailed my fingers through her hair and breathed her in. Before I knew what was happening, we were kissing again, and my arousal was insistent. Once again, I broke free, leaning my head back and gulping in air.

"I'm not so good at keeping my hands to myself when it comes to you," I said with a wry laugh.

Gemma pressed a hot kiss on the underside of my jaw. "Works for me," she said, her tone sly.

Before I knew it, she had unbuttoned my jeans and her palm was sliding around my cock. It was a testament to her persistence and my weakness for her. She moved so fast with only one hand that I couldn't even think clearly enough to protest. Next thing I knew, her mouth closed around the crown of my cock and she was sucking me into the warm depths.

It was a blur of heat and the slick suction of her

mouth. My release slammed through me before I could scramble to take control of the moment. Gemma rose up with a satisfied smile as her tongue swiped across her lips. "See, you didn't hurt me at all."

I mustered a glare, although it was weak. I persuaded her to shower with me, and there I teased her to her own climax with my fingers. Afterwards when we lounged on the couch, I called the resort to see who might be coming to town to bring me some clothes. Because I wasn't leaving Gemma's side, not tonight.

Chapter Thirty-Five

GEMMA

Four months later - Autumn

"How did I do?" I asked, exhausted relief coursing through me, a balm on my rattled nerves.

"Incredible," the DA said firmly.

His palms landed on my shoulders, his touch strong and reassuring. He guided me out of the court-room, where my parents and my brother were waiting. My brother dipped his head. "You handled that really well. I know it wasn't easy."

I stood still for a moment, feeling the wired stress unwind and ping through my body. I actually felt okay. Telling the truth had been much easier than I anticipated.

"How do you think it's going?" I asked my brother after hugs from both of my parents.

"I think it's going well. The DA told me they waited to file charges until they had a solid case. They definitely have a strong case. With as many witnesses that have come forward, I predict he might change

course and accept a plea deal. The mistake he made
was not doing that sooner because I don't think the
DA is going to do anything but play hardball with him
at this point."

I still couldn't believe the specter that had haunted
me ever since high school was finally banished. The
power of sunshine cast on dark secrets was strong
stuff. It was also amazing to realize I'd never been
alone. Some of the old wounds and friendships torn
apart in the aftermath of what happened to my high
school softball team had actually been healed. We
couldn't go back and do it all over, but we could share
in the relief of the truth coming to light and actual
consequences following.

EPILOGUE

Gemma

Six months later - Spring

Several months passed after the legal trial, and I felt like I'd fully closed the chapter on the part of my past I'd struggled to shake loose. My former coach had been convicted on multiple charges and was currently serving his sentence. The slice of my past was finally staying in the past, instead of the lingering after-effects chasing me into the future.

Diamond Creek felt like home for me now, and I loved it. I was at the bank with Diego, a decidedly unromantic setting. The woman helping us had stepped out of her office, leaving us alone while we waited.

I looked at Diego who was sitting beside me in a chair. "Are you sure about this?"

"Absolutely," he said without the slightest hesitation.

We were in here about to finalize the paperwork to purchase the home and property I'd been renting. The horses were included. Internally, I was kind of panicking. It felt very official, and we weren't even married yet.

I was suddenly awash in insecurity. I swallowed, trying to quell the anxiety tightening like a vise around my chest. I didn't realize my hands were cold and clammy until I felt his curl around one of mine where it rested on the sleek wooden armrest.

His grip was warm, strong, and sure, like everything about him. "Look at me, Gemma."

Angling toward him, my eyes were caught in the beam of his gaze. "Don't panic. Of course, I'm sure. I love you, and I plan to spend the rest my life with you. Buying a house together is just a detail. We're only doing this now because there was a competing offer on the property, so we needed to make a move, or let it go."

"You plan to spend the rest of your life with me?" I squeaked.

"I think we missed a step," he said, his thumb brushing back and forth across the back of my palm. Turning to face me more directly, he lifted my hand, turning it over and dropping a kiss in the center. "Will you marry me? I'm realizing just now it's been a given for me, but it seems I forgot to tell you that."

Then, I was laughing and crying, and he was asking me if that meant yes.

"Yes, yes!"

It was at that moment that the mortgage lady, as I'd come to call her in my mind, returned to her office. She stood stock still in the doorway, her hand resting on the doorknob. "Is everything okay?"

"Yes," I said more calmly this time.

Maybe it wasn't your typical romantic moment, but to me, signing page after page of documents seemed the absolute perfect thing to do immediately after you decided to get married. It felt like each signature was yet another sign of our commitment to each other.

———

DIEGO

More than three years later

I adjusted the angle of the plane in the air, taking a last glance out toward the mountains ahead, just before the wheels hit the runway below and the plane bounced slightly. I moved at record speed, getting the passengers off the plane and running through the after-flight checks before locking up the hangar and leaving for the evening.

These days I still loved my job, but I was always impatient to get home once I was out of the air. Thank God I had a boss who was kind enough to limit my overnight trips these last few months. Gemma was pregnant, and our baby was due soon.

I gunned it on the way home, smiling as I drove past the very place I'd picked up Gemma after Charlie threw her off a few years ago now. We still had Charlie, and he still occasionally threw her off. His streak of mischief ran wide and deep. I was profoundly relieved that Gemma's doctor had pointed out that she couldn't recommend riding a horse who was prone to throwing her off during her pregnancy. I thought I would've driven her insane with worry, if not for the saving grace of being busy with work.

Just as I turned into our driveway, my phone rang.

Seeing Gemma's name on my dashboard, I tapped the button as fast as I physically could. "What's up?"

"I'm at the hospital. My water broke early."

In a hot second, I was zipping through town, determined to get to the hospital before she actually had the baby. We still didn't know if it was a girl or a boy. We'd wanted the anticipation, but now all I could think about was whether or not Gemma would survive childbirth.

I flew through the hospital, almost plowing over Violet Hamilton. She called to my back as I dashed past her, "I'm fine!" even though my apology was a rushed call over my shoulder. "She's going to be fine!"

When I hurried into the room, Gemma met my eyes. "It's going really fast," she said between ragged breaths.

"Why is it going so fast?" I demanded of the doctor, as if that was a problem.

The doctor looked at me calmly. "Let's consider it a blessing. Your job is to support her."

Four hours later, I was acutely aware of why many people claimed women were stronger than men. I had no doubts about Gemma's strength, but my emotional fortitude was pushed to its limits. I truly had no clue how men got through this when labor lasted longer than that.

When our little boy let out a wail, and the doctor called me over to help cut the umbilical cord, my knees almost gave out. The next thing I remembered was resting my chin on Gemma's shoulder as she nursed our son for the first time. The hospital staff only managed to hold back my sisters for another hour.

Much as my sisters could be nosy and interfering, they were a godsend after we returned home. In my spare time, I'd renovated the upstairs of the barn into a guest apartment. All four of my sisters stayed with us for weeks. They cooked meals for us and basically took care of all the logistics while Gemma and I settled into being new parents.

"You've got this, Diego," Harley said.

I was holding our son with one hand and carefully heating up a bottle filled with Gemma's breastmilk with the other. We'd named him Jacob after my father.

"Do you think?"

Just then, Gemma came out of the bedroom, her footsteps quiet on the floor as she crossed the kitchen to us.

Harley winked at me and disappeared out the kitchen door, leaving me with my small family, my entire world.

"Of course, you have this," Gemma murmured, leaning up to dust a kiss across my lips.

"I'm not so sure sometimes." Having a child gave new meaning to uncertainty. It was both exhilarating and terrifying.

"Absolutely," Gemma said firmly. "We're going to stumble through this together."

I encircled her with my free arm, and it literally felt as if a lock clicked into place when I held my son in one arm with Gemma pressed to my side. Everything was exactly the way it was supposed to be. The only way I wanted it.

Thank you for reading Come To Me - I hope you loved Diego & Gemma's story!

Up next in the Dare With Me Series is Nora & Gabriel's story!

Gabriel is off limits. For good reason. He's best friends with Nora's older brother. He's also smoldering, sexy, and waaayyyy too tempting.

They think they can keep it a secret. They think they can pull off the friends-with-benefits thing. Spoiler alert: they can't.

It's only after Nora stops talking to Gabriel that he discovers just how much it hurts to break his own heart.

This brooding, sexy, ex-military pilot needs to find a way to win back the one and only woman who stole his heart.

Don't miss Gabriel & Nora's epic second chance, hate to love romance!

Pre-order Back To Us

For more swoon-worthy small town romance...

This Crazy Love kicks off the Swoon Series - small town southern romance with enough heat to melt you! Jackson & Shay's story is epic - swoon-worthy & intensely emotional. Jackson just happens to be Shay's brother's best friend. He's also *seriously* easy on the eyes. Shay has a past, the kind of past she would most definitely like to forget. Past or not, Jackson is about to rock her world. Don't miss their story! Free on all retailers!

Burn For Me is a second chance romance for the ages. Sexy firefighters? Check. Rugged men? Check. Wrapped up together? Check. Brave the fire in this hot, small-town romance. Amelia & Cade were high school sweethearts & then it all fell apart. When they cross paths again, it's epic - don't miss Cade's story!
Free on all retailers!

For more small town romance, take a visit to Last Frontier Lodge in Diamond Creek. A sexy, alpha SEAL meets his match with a brainy heroine in Take Me Home. Marley is all brains & Gage is all brawn. Sparks fly when their worlds collide. Don't miss Gage & Marley's story!
Free on all retailers!

If sports romance lights your spark, check out The Play. Liam is a British footballer who falls for Olivia, his doctor. A twist of forbidden heats up this swoon-worthy & laugh-out-loud romance. Don't miss Liam & Olivia's story.
Free on all retailers!

Sign up for my newsletter, so you can receive information about upcoming new releases & receive a FREE copy of one of my books: http:// jhcroixauthor.com/subscribe/

FIND MY BOOKS

Thank you for reading Come To Me! I hope you enjoyed the story. If so, you can help other readers find my books in a variety of ways.

1) Write a review!

2) Sign up for my newsletter, so you can receive information about upcoming new releases & receive a FREE copy of one of my books: http:// jhcroixauthor.com/subscribe/

3) Like and follow my Amazon Author page at https:// amazon.com/author/jhcroix

4) Follow me on Bookbub at https://www.bookbub. com/authors/j-h-croix

5) Follow me on Instagram at https://www. instagram.com/jhcroix/

6) Like my Facebook page at https://www. facebook.com/jhcroix

Dare With Me Series

Crash Into You

Evers & Afters

Come To Me

Back To Us - coming June 2021!

Swoon Series

This Crazy Love

Wait For Me

Break My Fall

Truly Madly Mine

Still Go Crazy

If We Dare

Steal My Heart

Into The Fire Series

Burn For Me

Slow Burn

Burn So Bad

Hot Mess

Burn So Good

Sweet Fire

Play With Fire

Melt With You

Burn For You

Crash & Burn

That Snowy Night

Brit Boys Sports Romance

The Play

Big Win

Out Of Bounds

Play Me

Naughty Wish

Diamond Creek Alaska Novels

When Love Comes

Follow Love

Love Unbroken

Love Untamed
Tumble Into Love
Christmas Nights
Last Frontier Lodge Novels
Take Me Home
Love at Last
Just This Once
Falling Fast
Stay With Me
When We Fall
Hold Me Close
Crazy For You
Just Us

ACKNOWLEDGMENTS

Hugs & kisses to all of my readers. Every story is a leap of faith, and your support gives me the courage to keep writing.

My assistant makes it possible for me to focus on my stories, and she's incredibly patient on top of it. Much gratitude to my editor for helping me polish the story and to Terri D. for her detail skills. Hugs my early readers and to the bloggers who share the news about my books.

During a long and challenging year—sheesh—I'm deeply grateful for my husband, for my family, for my friends, and for my dogs.

xoxo

J.H. Croix

ABOUT THE AUTHOR

USA Today Bestselling Author J. H. Croix lives in a small town in the historical farmlands of Maine with her husband and two spoiled dogs. Croix writes contemporary romance with sassy women and alpha men who aren't afraid to show some emotion. Her love for quirky small-towns and the characters that inhabit them shines through in her writing. Take a walk on the wild side of romance with her bestselling novels!

Places you can find me:
jhcroixauthor.com
jhcroix@jhcroix.com

f facebook.com/jhcroix
o instagram.com/jhcroix
BB bookbub.com/authors/j-h-croix

Made in the USA
Las Vegas, NV
08 July 2021

26139723R00138